brews & bartenders

katrina marie

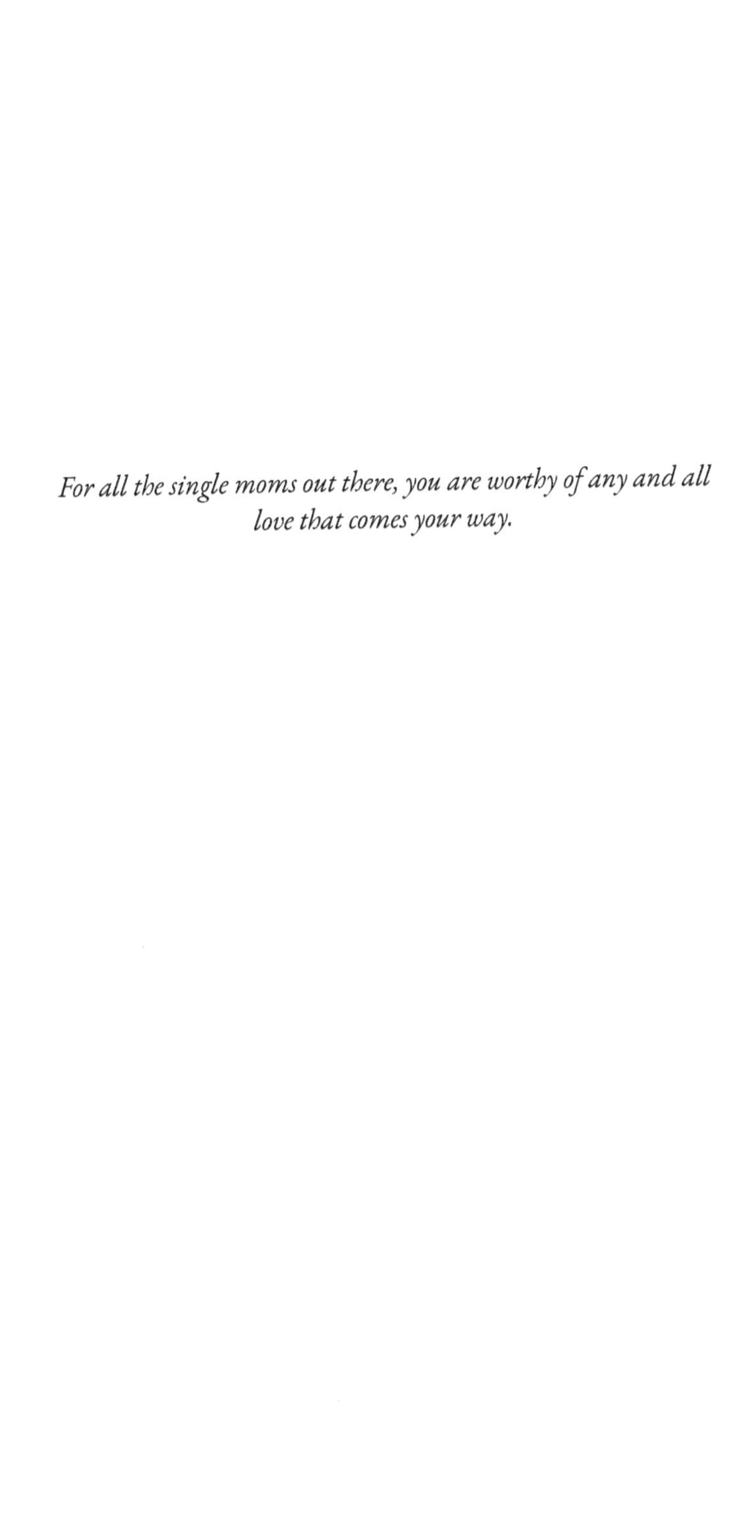

For all the single moms out there, you are worthy of any and all love that comes your way.

prologue

THE DOOR SLAMS with a finality I never imagined I'd have to go through. But here I am. Staring through teary eyes at the door.

This isn't how I pictured my life. My son crying in my arms while the man I thought I would spend the rest of my life with, walks out the door without a backward glance. No goodbyes, or we can work on things. Just gone.

Being a single mom is not what I had in mind when I said 'I do.' To make matters worse, I can't afford this house on my own. Without another source of income, I'll be forced to move back in with Mom. Disrupting the routine she has with Reaf and Bryce.

No. I will *not* do that. I don't need to figure it all out right now, but I will soon. Full-time job and everything. It's the only thing that will provide for us. I'm not sure what is going through Nathan's head, but I need to do what is best for me and my child. If he comes around and wants to make this work, I'll consider it. Even if it's against my better judgement. If he was willing to do the work in the first place, he wouldn't have walked out the door.

Standing, I walk around and pat David's back. He's teething and there isn't much that will calm him down, but I'm hoping the movement will help. It has to at some point.

So many thoughts are running through my mind, and I can't keep any of them straight.

I quit my job toward the end of my pregnancy, and I doubt they'll take me back. They made it pretty clear where they stood when I told them I wanted time with my son because six weeks of maternity leave wasn't enough. They didn't bat an eye when I left. It was then I realized they weren't as family friendly as I'd hoped.

David finally dozes off, and I bend over to place him in the pack 'n' play. There's a knock at the door and I jump, waking him up.

His cries are deafening as I head toward the door. I have no idea who it could be. If it was Nathan, with a change of heart, he would have walked in, right?

Readjusting David to my shoulder, I open the door and sigh in relief. It's not Nathan, but someone even better.

"Mom." The word comes out as a sob, and she rushes in, dropping the bags of takeout, and wraps her arms around me.

"What's the matter? Did I get my days mixed up again?"

"What?" Too much has happened today, and I can't process what she's saying.

"Dinner," she says, letting go of me. "It's Tuesday, right? Our weekly dinner night."

She pulls David from my arms, and by some sort of magic, he calms down the instant he's cradled in her arms. "I'm sorry, I completely forgot."

Taking in my appearance, she glances around the house. All the rooms are dark except the foyer we're in and the living room. "Where's Nathan?"

That question does me in. I walk to the couch and sag into the cushions, trying to hold back my sobs, but the tears run down my cheeks. Traitorous emotions. Why can't I be sad, or only angry?

I know he left less than an hour ago, but rage and despair fill my every fiber. I don't even know where to begin, so I start with the simple answer. "He left."

"Like he went to the store?"

"No, Mom." I shake my head and take a deep breath. "As in walked out on me. On David. Our little family."

David has fallen asleep in her arms and she lays him down before sitting beside me, and pulling me into her arms once more. "I'm so sorry, sweetie."

"I don't know what I'm going to do, Mom." I sniffle into her arm. "I quit my job to be home with him and focus on our family. Now, I don't have a choice but to go back to work."

"We'll figure it out."

"I shouldn't have to. He was it for me. I don't know what I did to make him leave."

She leans back and lifts my chin until my eyes meet hers. "You did *nothing* wrong. Him leaving has nothing to do with you, and everything to do with him."

"All he said before packing his bags and walking out the door, was that he wasn't cut out for this life. And that he wasn't ready to be a family man." I shake my head, trying to make it make sense. "It came out of left field. We were both on board with trying for David."

"Nobody truly knows what is going through his head, but him. You can't beat yourself up about it." She waits a few moments for me to get myself under control. "Is this what you want? That's the important thing. I'm here for you whether you're done with him or willing to give him another chance. If he comes to his senses, that is."

"I don't know." It's the only answer I have.

"Pack a bag for you and David."

"What? Why?"

"Because I don't think you should be alone right now. You can stay in the guest room for a few days until you get your bearings. Then decide what you want to do."

I shake my head. "I can't do that. Reaf and Bryce shouldn't have their schedules interrupted because my husband decided he'd rather have freedom from us."

There's the anger again. It's like a pendulum swinging back and forth. Sadness and mourning to intense rage. I don't know if it'll ever stop. If I'll ever feel normal again.

"Don't you worry about them." She stands and leads me down the hall. "They can handle anything. Who knows? Maybe they'll enjoy having you around for a bit."

"Yeah, because nothing says cool teenager like hanging out with your older sister and nephew."

"Don't be like that," she scoffs. "Just get your bags ready. I'll grab the food and take it to the car."

I feel horrible our weekly dinner was ruined. It's not my fault, but I'm certain this mess isn't what she imagined walking into. At least, I don't think it's my fault. It could be and he was just giving me a bullshit answer to keep me from feeling bad.

A small part of me wonders if there is someone else. Someone who isn't overstimulated and exhausted after a day of taking care of a baby. Someone who can give him what I obviously can't when I pass out after David goes to sleep.

Mom must see the dark thoughts enter my mind. She must have had the same ones before Dad left. "Don't go there." She gives my arm a small squeeze before letting go. "Both of you need time to think. Giving in to your worst fears isn't going to help matters."

Easier said than done. She leaves me to pack and I can't help from going there once again. It's a black hole I should avoid, but it's difficult when it's consuming my mind.

In an effort to distract myself, I make a list of things we'll need. Ticking each one off mentally as I add them to a bag. It helps...sort of.

With my bag done, I set it outside our bedroom door. No, not ours. I don't know that it'll ever be that again. I can't dwell on it right now. I need to get through the task at hand. When we get to Mom's, I can grab a bottle of wine and drown my sorrows. David will be in capable hands, and I can let myself break down.

I head across the hallway to David's room. I throw as many clothes as I can into a bag. Grab a box of diapers and some of his favorite toys. My bag is already gone from the hall when I leave his room. Mom must have snuck back here to get it.

When I get to the living room, she has David strapped in his car seat. "I need to grab some bottles and formula."

"I already did," Mom reassures me. "If you think of anything else you need before you're ready to come back here, we can take a trip to the store." She pauses while I take in the house, we've made our home. "Are you ready?"

No. Not even close. I gaze around the rooms. Already they feel empty. Love is no longer filling the space. Only despair and heartache. I'm not sure what the future will hold. Reunion or parenting as a single mom? Only time will tell.

For now, I'm lucky it all happened tonight. Lucky my mom remembered our dinner night, and showed up at the front door when I needed her most. With one last look, I nod my head. "I'm ready."

1

caroline

GEEZ, I need to remember I'm not as young as I used to be. Not that I went out much then. I was too busy trying to build a life with Nathan. That obviously didn't work out.

Out of the Ashes is modern and old at the same time. I remember when Angie's uncle owned the place before he passed away. I was still a teenager, but everyone knew this place.

It's right on the edge of downtown Asheville. I can't count how many times some group of nay-sayers tried to get it shut down. In their opinion, the clientele wasn't savory, and they didn't want that sort of trouble so close to the boutiques. It never went through. Thank goodness. If it had we'd have nowhere close by to hang out. We'd have to drive an hour to Dallas, or go to one of the neighboring towns. Since high school rivalries are a thing, none of us do that too often.

"Hey," Sam nudges my shoulder. "I'm going to grab us another drink. What do you want?"

"Surprise me." I grin. It's one of the few nights I can kick back and relax with my friends. I love David with all my heart. He's my reason for living, but sometimes a mom needs a little me time.

"You shouldn't have told her that," Kate laughs. "She's going to come back with something that will knock you on your ass."

I shrug. If she does, I'll call my mom or Reaf to come pick me up. Hell, I'll ask Bryce if I have to. Actually, that's a good idea. I've already had a couple of drinks and there's no way I'm getting behind the wheel.

Pulling out my phone, I shoot off a text to my baby brother. He's honestly the best option. Assuming he isn't somewhere hanging out with his friends. It's been a whole semester since he's seen them and I remember how that felt all too well.

Bryce: You got it.
Caroline: You don't have plans?
Bryce: Not until this weekend. Everyone is being respectable and looking for summer jobs.
Caroline: Okay. Thank you broski.
Bryce: Have a fun kid free night.
Bryce: And don't ever call me that again. Lame.

Laughing, I put my phone back in my pocket. He may act like he hates the nickname, but I think he secretly loves it. Once Reaf and Tonya got married, he and I became closer than I ever thought. I'm honestly not sure how I would have handled being home with only mom all the time. I mean, she's been amazing since the divorce, but nothing says spinster like hanging out with your mom on Friday nights.

"Please tell me whoever you're texting isn't related to you." Emily comes around the high-top table and gives me a hug.

"I was arranging for my brother to pick me up when we're

done here. Thank you very much." I push her away. "It's about time you showed up."

"Sorry," she grimaces. "My mom called and you know how she can be. Always meddling and trying to set me up with one of her friends' sons. It's annoying."

I shudder at the thought. My mom tried that once and after my reaction, never did it again. I don't want anything long term. Or well, even short term. Taking care of a kid and working full time has me busy enough. Nights like this are my one indulgence.

"So, any cute guys from out of town come in?" Emily sets her wallet on the table and waves at Sam. "Please tell me she went up there for a refill. I need a drink after all that nonsense."

"Yep," Kate laughs. "You can have mine since I'm sure she already ordered our drinks. I'll go grab my own. You need to catch up."

"It's not like we didn't see each other earlier today." I shake my head. "I mean we do work together."

"True," Emily taps the table. "The only difference is, that was work time. *This* is our playtime."

"You make it sound so dirty." Kate takes the final drink from her glass before heading to the bar to help Sam and get another drink.

"So, are you going to find some trouble tonight?"

I hate the fact this question gets brought up every week. We all went to school together. We lost touch after Nathan and I got married. Even back then, when he and I were high school sweethearts, they never liked him.

Once they found out we were heading for divorce and I needed a job, they didn't hesitate to hire me on at the floral business they had recently started together. It took a while to take off, but with small town weddings becoming popular, we occasionally have to turn people away now.

"Are we really going to do this again?"

"You never know. You could find "Mister Right" in this very bar. But you'll never know because you don't put yourself out there."

"Honestly, who in their right mind would want to date a woman that comes with baggage."

"Your brother did."

"He's an exception to the rule. Reaf has always been wise beyond his years."

Sam and Kate are back at the table, efficiently putting an end to the conversation. "What did we miss?" Sam sets a drink in front of me and another one in front of Emily.

"Oh, nothing." Emily takes a sip of her drink before making a face. "Why does this taste like tequila?"

"Oh shit," Sam covers her mouth. "That was for Caroline."

"Oh no. I did *not* ask for tequila."

"You told me to surprise you." She holds her hands in the air and wiggles her fingers. "Surprise!"

"How about I go grab another beer, and you take this one?"

"You're no fun," Sam pouts.

"Yes, I am," I laugh as I turn from the table. "I just don't need tequila to make me that way."

The three of them are giggling as I walk away from the table. I can only imagine what they're talking about as soon as I'm out of earshot. Probably figuring out who they are going to set me up with. And Emily talks about her mom meddling. Those three are just as bad. If not worse.

Even though it's a Wednesday, Out of the Ashes is busier than normal. I weave through groups dancing to the music coming through the speaker. The space they have next door needs to hurry up and be done. Then these people can go over there and those of us who only want to hang out can occupy this side. I don't have anything against dancing, but I've been almost knocked over too many times to count.

Finding an empty spot at the bar is close to impossible, but the second one opens up, I squeeze in. I'm not loud enough to be heard over multiple people.

A guy, younger than me, leans over to take my order. I open my mouth but he's redirected before I can even speak. Now, Carlos, the head bartender, is standing in front of me. A tall glass of beer in front of him.

"Is that for me?" I can't help the blush I'm sure is present.

"Yes." Short and to the point. "I got it ready as soon as I noticed you coming this way. I tried talking your friend out of the drink she got you, but she didn't listen."

"Thank you." I reach for the glass and our fingers meet for the briefest moment. He's attractive, and if I didn't have a little person that depended on me, I'd probably ask him on a date. But I do, and there's no point.

When I turn back toward the table, I notice all three of my friends staring in my direction. The second they see me looking back, they turn around. Why do I feel like I was just set up?

Sam has a shit-eating grin when I get back to my side of the table. "You ordered that drink on purpose, didn't you?"

"Maybe."

I point a finger at Kate. "Did you know?"

She shrugs and doesn't say a word. She totally knew. I don't know why they are so fixated on me finding someone. I've told them time and time again that I have zero interest.

"Don't be mad," Kate finally says. "But we know you think he's hot, even if he is a little older."

"And," Sam butts in. "From the way he's always looking at you, he feels the same."

"It doesn't matter," I throw my hands in the air, inches from hitting a waitress walking behind me. "I don't want any sort of relationship. I've got David to think about. And right now, it hits a little harder than normal."

"Oh shit," Emily gasps. "I completely forgot it's almost the anniversary of that time."

Yeah, that's putting it mildly. It's been almost six years since Nathan and I have split up. I don't still harbor feelings for him, but he's already been remarried and divorced since then. He could move on so quickly. And to this day I can't find it in me to trust anyone else.

"Yeah." The good time I was having is brought down by the mention of my ex. You'd think I'd be over it by now, but the sting of rejection is something I still feel. It's one of the reasons I don't date. The other reason is hopefully asleep with my mom watching over him.

"Sorry," Emily whispers. "I didn't mean to bring it front and center." The music is loud and the people yelling to be heard at the tables next to us make it hard to hear what she's said, but I get the gist.

"It's all good." I plaster a fake smile across my face. My friends see right through it. They keep their mouths closed, though. Willing to fake it right along with me. "Let's not mention horrible exes for the rest of the night. I still have a bit before my baby brother will be here to pick me up, and we're here to have a good time."

"Speaking of baby brothers," Kate waggles her eyebrows up and down. "Is he single?"

I choke on the drink I just took and almost spit beer everywhere. "You are not dating my baby brother." I wipe my mouth in case any liquid managed to escape. "Remember, we had a rule, no siblings."

"Yeah, yeah," Kate waves my words away. "I know. No siblings. In my defense, you shouldn't have good looking brothers."

"Gross." I groan. "Okay, let's move on from that subject."

I know she's only doing it to get under my skin, but it still grosses me out. They are my brothers. She's never had to worry about that aspect with her friends liking her siblings. She's an only child. The rest of us know the feeling all too well.

"Okay," Sam snorts. "Can we talk about the wedding for the bridezilla we have coming up?"

"I'm guessing she made more changes?" I sigh.

"Yep," Emily crosses her arms on the table. "She called right after you left asking us if we could change the flower type."

"You told her no, right?"

Kate is already shaking her head. "Nope. We did say that this was the last change."

"That's good, at least." We've got to get the contract updated to say no changes so many days before a wedding.

"We may need to cancel next week's hangout, though." Emily groans.

That's going to suck, but I get it. Their, no our, first priority is the client. The shop is finally getting some buzz, and we need to do whatever we can to keep that coming. Now if I could remember I'm an actual part of the team, and not someone they pity.

Sam taps the table with her knuckles. "One last round before we head home?"

"Yes," we all say in unison.

"But nothing heavy for me. I still have to get David ready for school," I add.

Sam mutters something about weekends when she leaves the table. They'll understand when they have kids. Aside from the flower shop, David is my biggest priority. And he always will be.

2

carlos

"IT LOOKS like it's going to be a busy night." Eric taps the bar top with his knuckles. "Are you here all night?"

One day my coworkers will realize I don't do small talk. I'm here to work and nothing else. "Yeah. Angie is taking the night off."

"Any of the other bartenders coming in tonight?"

He always has questions. As if he's the one in charge. I know what nights to schedule more staff. Wednesday through Saturday night, like clockwork. "Yep. We won't need them for a couple of hours."

"You sure about that?" He points toward the front of the bar. The door opens and another large group walks in.

Damn. He's right. I may need to call them in earlier. We rarely get hit with a rush like this. At least, not this early. "Let's see how the next hour goes. If we are swamped, we'll call them in."

"Okay," he nods. "I'll grab this side and you grab the other?"

"Sure." Quickly, I look over the area, making sure everything is in order. It's perfection. I didn't work last night, and it's good to know my bar staff put things away the way I taught them.

Delilah, Lisa's friend, leads them to a table in the back. It's the only table big enough to fit them. I feel bad for whoever has their table. They've been in here a few times and get loud.

"So, do you think she'll show up tonight?" Eric asks as he grabs a bottle of vodka and takes it to his side of the bar.

I know who he's talking about, but I don't want to give voice to his question. I hope *she* comes tonight. She always makes an appearance with her friends. Every Wednesday, like clockwork. Tonight, won't be any different. And I won't get the nerve to talk to her either.

"Maybe," I shrug. That's all I'll say about the subject. They all know I like her. Not a night goes by, when she's here, they don't give me crap about not asking her on a date.

I wonder if it's illegal for me to fire my bartenders for picking on me. I hear Eric laugh, and it only makes me want to look up the information even more. None of my employees take me seriously. At least, not anymore. When they first started working here, they were terrified to speak to me. Now...I'm the ass of their jokes. When did that happen?

Eric strides back to my side of the bar. "When she comes in, I'll cover your area. You need to grow a pair and ask her out."

"You need to shut up before you lose your job." I grunt. The audacity of these kids. Forcing my hand through my hair, I sigh. For once, I'm hoping she doesn't come in. Eric has thrown down the gauntlet, and I'll never live it down if I don't make the attempt. This is the day I become a softie. When I allow my twenty-something year old coworkers to bully me into something I'm too scared to do on my own.

Laughter follows behind Eric as he heads toward a

customer. "You won't fire me. Who else would brighten your day the way I do?"

"I don't know about that." Though gruff, my voice doesn't carry. It's a good thing my sisters never come in, otherwise they'd be joining in this ridiculous notion.

Another rush of people gather at the door. Damn, Eric was right. I need to call the other bartenders in earlier. There's going to be another line outside.

I'll be happy when the other room is fully open. We'll need more staff again, but at least people won't be waiting outside. They get impatient and get an attitude towards my people.

A few more months. I have to keep telling myself that. Delilah shoots me a worried glance as she leads the large group to a table. Her hint they may be a rowdy bunch.

Even if Caroline comes in with her friends tonight, I won't have time to approach her. I guess the universe delivers small favors.

* * *

"Hey, Boss," Eric grins. "Looks like you gotta pay the piper."

As if I didn't know Caroline was here. The moment she walked through the door, she caught my attention. My gaze was on her as she waited for Delilah to lead her to a table. And when she sat down at a table close to the bar. Her group of friends isn't with her. That's a small relief. If I make my move, at least I won't make an ass of myself in front of all of them.

I wave my hand over the bar. "In case you haven't noticed, we have a full bar. I can't exactly go over there and leaving all our customers hanging."

"Sure, you can." He pours a glass of wine. "You ask one of us lowly bartenders to cover for you. Then you walk over there and ask her on a damn date."

I'm not responding to that. I grab another glass as one of our regulars approaches the bar and holds up a finger. He doesn't even have to say what he wants before I hand over his whiskey and coke.

This is the service I want all of my staff to have. We have new people come in frequently, but most of our clientele are folks that live here in town. If we keep them happy, they have nothing to complain about. It's one of the reasons we don't have too many issues about keeping the bar open. At least, not since Angie took over and Stella helped with rebranding.

Speaking of, Angie pushes her way past the crowd and leans against the bar. She's not even supposed to be here. "What are you doing here? I didn't think you were on the schedule."

She shrugs. "Dylan has poker night with the guys and I had nothing better to do."

"So, you come to work?"

"It looks like it's a good thing I did. We're slammed tonight."

"No more than usual." And it's not. Wednesday is for our wine drinkers. Discount wine always brings people in. "We have it covered."

"How about you take a break and I cover your end of the bar?" She glances over my shoulder and I turn to see Eric grinning.

They are ganging up on me. Did this fool text her? "I don't need a break."

She walks off. Hopefully going to her office to do something that doesn't concern me. A tap on my shoulder a few moments later proves otherwise. "I said I don't need a break. The longer you interrupt me, the longer it will take me to pour these drinks."

"Why are you such an ass?" Angie puts her hands on her

hips and glares at me. I swear one day she's going to terrify her own kids with that look. "I'm trying to help you, but no. You'd rather work."

"I didn't ask for your help, Ang." I grunt. "And I know you giving me a break isn't for anything other than ulterior motives."

"I don't know what you mean." She crosses her arms over her chest.

"You know exactly what I mean." I point toward Eric, who has been watching our interaction. He turns when he sees me looking at him. "Eric texted you with his little scheme and you came running to aid him because you can't help yourself."

Hiring him may have been a bad decision. The two of them are like partners in crime. If something is awry, it usually has their names written all over it. It was bad enough when Lisa was here playing matchmaker. Now it's even worse. If it isn't my bar crew putting pressure on me to make a move, it's Angie.

As much as I'd like to ask Caroline on a date, I can't. I'm Angie's partner in this business. She did it on her own for so long, and I agreed to pick up the slack. How is that going to be possible if there is someone taking my attention away from the bar? Not to mention the days I go see my family. There are only so many ways I can divide and compartmentalize myself.

"Look," Angie finally speaks up. "I know it's not ideal with the way the bar is growing. But you deserve some happiness. It's not like she has a ton of spare time, either."

"What do you mean?"

"She has a kid, and he takes up most of her time." She eyes me. "How did you not know that?"

"It never came up when she ordered her beer."

"Yeah, but her brother is in here all the time. I'm almost certain he's mentioned his nephew a few times."

If she thinks I listen in on conversations, she's crazy. I

barely have room for the thoughts in my own head. I don't need to hear anyone else's. "I must have missed it."

"Gee, don't sound too excited."

I know she probably thinks I'm an asshole. Caroline having a kid changes nothing about my interest in her. It just makes a complicated situation more complicated. "I'm working. What do you want me to do?"

"We want you to ask her out already."

"And if she shoots me down?" How am I not going to let that affect me? "She's here every week, and I'm usually the bartender working. It'll be awkward."

"It's better than being a coward." Damn, she's not pulling any punches tonight.

"Okay." My voice dripping with defeat. They will not let this go until I do something about it. Might as well get it over with. "But not right now."

"Soon." The crowd at the bar has grown, and it's going to take all of us to get it back under control.

With all hands on deck, everyone has a drink in their hands within ten minutes. There's a small lull, and one of the new waitstaff comes to the bar to give us an order. I can't remember her name, and I feel kind of shitty about it. But what can I do? Even though the hiring process is tighter, some people aren't cut out for customer service.

Eric intercepts her and grins. "Looks like the woman you've been lusting over needs a drink." He nods his head in her direction. Why does he have to make me sound like a lovesick teen? I've been in relationships before. They require more time than I have. But I'll do it if only to prove to them it'll be a failure.

She's leaning back against the wall, a book in her hand, without a care in the world. Her whole mood is different than when she's with her friends. More serene and less chaotic.

"What about her waitress?"

"She's on board. It's not like you'll be taking her every drink. Just. This. One."

"Fine." I grab a mug and set it under the tap. It's a good thing I know what she prefers to drink. I grab a lime out of the bin and slip it on the lip of the mug. "Here goes nothing," I mutter.

Angie gives me a thumbs up as I make my way to the end of the bar. My hand holding the beer mug shakes and I take a deep breath. My steps are slow and measured. Am I taking my time? Yes. I don't want to look like an idiot.

The people seated at the bar watch me. Unfortunately, they know what I'm about to do. Some of them are nodding their approval while others are doing their best to hold in their laughter. Great. I'm a joke to these people.

Caroline isn't paying attention to me. Her sole focus on the story in her hands. Less than ten steps. That's all I need to get to her table. A part of me wants to turn around. Forget this whole thing and act like my coworkers aren't assholes for pushing me into this.

The chatter in the bar fades to nothing. Surely, they aren't all watching me? Or maybe I'm imagining the quiet. In my own head more often than I should be. Especially at a time like this.

One foot in front of the other. Am I sweating? Probably. I'll blame it on so many people being in here. It's not my nerves at all.

Five steps. Four. Three. Two.

Someone darts between her table and me. My foot hits their shoe and I go forward. The beer tipping forward in slow motion. Oh shit. This is not the impression I wanted to make.

The person stops and I hear words, but I can't make them out. All I see is the beer flying toward the woman I've become infatuated with.

Caroline looks up, lets go of her book, and scoots out of the way. Every action seems to take minutes, though I know it's only seconds. Beer sloshes all over her book, and I feel like a moron.

3

caroline

"I'M SO SORRY." The words are on repeat. Carlos has a rag in his hand, trying to mop up the mess he's made. The edges of my book are soaking wet. Guess I'll have to pay the damage fees for that now.

"It's fine." The words are harsher than I intend.

So far, it's been one thing after another today. Nathan was supposed to pick up David and canceled at the last minute. I don't think anyone realizes how hard it is to come up with excuses for your ex-husband to keep your child from hurting. It's not David's fault his father is selfish.

Luckily, baby brother stepped up and offered to babysit for me. I'm honestly shocked he did it, but grateful all the same.

Carlos is still cleaning up the mess, and I feel like I should help. I mean, he did it. At the same time, I shouldn't stand over him brooding like a brat.

He's mopping up the mess. "I've never done that before. This guy stepped in front of me and I tripped."

"No, really. It's fine." I grab a few napkins off the table and dab at the wet spots on the chair. I'm still annoyed, but it's not like he did it on purpose.

"I'll buy you a new book." He lifts it up to inspect the damage. "Well, I'll pay the library fee for it. I'm sure they'll have to replace it now."

He's flustered and it's a look I've never seen on him before. He's usually gruff and serious. His cheeks might even be blushing. It's hard to tell against his tan skin. A part of me wants to laugh at the whole circumstance, but this is my one night out and nothing is going my way.

"It's really not a big deal." Though, now I'm curious why he's the one who brought my drink. I've seen him serve customers before, but never when the bar is this packed. That's what the rest of the employees are for. "What happened to the person who was waiting on me?"

"She went on break." He waves his hand toward someone behind the bar, and they nod. A few moments later one of the employee's hands him a mop and disappears. I also see the girl who was taking my order, carry a tray to a table on the other side of the room. He's lying.

"I'm going to," I point toward the bathroom, "clean up." My hands are sticky from the beer and I want to make sure I don't have any wet spots on me. I definitely don't want to look like I peed my pants. This will also give me time to figure out what he's doing serving drinks instead of pouring them behind the bar.

"Go ahead. I'll have this cleaned up before you get back and a new drink in place." He continues to mop the area around the table.

Pushing my way through the crowd, I enter the bathroom at the end of the hall. There's a line. Of course, there is. Because why would anything work in my favor today? I debate pushing my way past the people in line to the mirror, but I know that will only piss people off. Getting in an argument isn't on my list of things to do today. Especially after everything that has happened. I can't say it would work in my favor. It's almost like Friday the 13th bad luck, but on a day that is neither Friday nor the thirteenth.

The line moves along slowly, giving me time to be with my thoughts. Every part of my brain is working through the day. First, waking up well after my alarm went off. The bride from hell making last minute changes to her bouquets. I should be helping my friends instead of here at the bar. Then Nathan calling at the last possible second to cancel his plans with our son. Which left me with coming up with yet another excuse to give David because his dad can't be bothered to spend any sort of quality time with him. Luckily my mom and Bryce stepped up to take care of him tonight. Much like they always do. I'm not sure where I'd be without them.

All I wanted was a nice night out to decompress. Drink a couple of beers and read my book. Pathetic? Maybe, but it got me out of the house. Maybe I should have gone to Brews Clues and stuck to coffee. No, I wanted to come here. It's the norm for me. Wednesday nights at Out of the Ashes with my girls. And now...my book is ruined and my clothes may be wet in unfortunate places.

Finally, the mirror is in front of me and I step out of the line to check my clothes. There's the spot on my knee and a few drops on my shirt. Turning, I look over my shoulder to make sure none got on the back of me. Nothing. At least that's going my way tonight.

I face the mirror once again, checking my makeup. My lipstick is still intact, eye makeup is good. Hell, I don't know why I'm checking. It's not like I'm here to meet anyone. I don't have time for that. I have a son waiting at home. One who is in sports and needs me to be focused completely on him.

Maybe having beer spilled on me is a sign I need to go home. To spend time with my kid and not take a moment for granted. Not be here in this bar, checking out the bartender when he's not looking. Because let's be honest, that's why I'm here. I find Carlos attractive. It's the reason I'm here early when the girls are with me. All so I have a chance to ogle him without them giving me shit. But I don't understand why he went out of his way to bring me my drink tonight. It's unlike him, not that I know him all that well, but I've observed enough to know it's not the norm. And I need to know the answer.

Now that I've confirmed I don't look like a hot mess, I can get to the bottom of this. People move out of my way as I walk through the bathroom to the door. Apparently, I look like a woman on a mission. Not that I'm complaining. It's less people I have to force my way through.

I don't see Carlos as I approach the table I was occupying, but the person who originally took my order is setting another glass of beer on the table. A lime wedged on the lip of the glass. If she had brought my drink originally, none of this would have happened.

I take a seat and grab the beer. The glass is cold as it meets my lips. The small sip enough to repair my mood. Not by much. Enough to keep me from marching to the bar and demanding Carlos tell me what exactly is going on. Except when I look toward the bar area, he's not there. The only people I notice are Angie, the owner, and another bartender I've never met before. Both of them are staring in my direction. I can't understand why, though. Did I have something on my face and miss it? God, I hope not.

I look away and take another sip of my beer. I notice my book is gone. Maybe, Carlos has it? I'm not sure, but I'm definitely going to need it back. Despite it being ruined, I will have to return it to the library.

A chair slides across the floor and stops right beside me. The book lands with a heavy thump on the table. "Angie keeps a blow dryer in the office. I thought I'd try to dry it as much as possible. But I'll still pay for it if I need to. It's my fault."

Carlos's voice is deep and full of regret. I can't help but feel bad for him. He sounds completely torn up about the spilled drink. I pick up the book and flip through the pages. Some of them are still damp, but it's not completely horrible now. "You didn't have to do that." I glance up into his brown eyes and his gaze is intense. "Thank you, though."

"Not a problem."

He stands to leave but I place a hand on his. I don't know why I do it, but it's almost instinct. "Can I ask you a question?"

"Sure."

He glances toward the bar then back at me. He's chewing on his bottom lip. Whatever he thinks is about to come out of my mouth makes him nervous. He's not the only one. "Why were you the one who served me the last drink? Not that I'm upset about it. You rarely leave the bar, especially when it's packed."

He side steps the question with one of his own. "Why aren't your friends here? You're usually with them."

Maybe if I answer his question, he'll answer mine. I'm going to try it and hope it doesn't blow up in my face. "They are getting things together for a wedding this weekend. They said they didn't need my help, and to keep our original plans. So," I lift my arms in the air, "here I am. Now answer my question."

His focus is no longer on me. Eyes going to every part of the building. Anything to keep from falling on me again. "Carlos?"

"Yeah?"

"Why did you bring me the drink instead of the normal staff?"

He mumbles something too low for me to hear, but clears his throat and speaks. "You've been coming here for months, and I've noticed."

"Okay." That doesn't sound creepy at all. "But what does that have to do with anything?"

"I, um, was wondering if you'd go out on a date with me."

That was not what I was expecting. I don't even know what to say. He caught me completely off guard. I open my mouth, but can't form words. This isn't good. I can't date anyone. Especially not him. I've already proved to my friends and myself that I like him. That I find him attractive. I know it could never be one date with this guy. I would want more and more. I can't do that. Not now, anyway. Not when I have David to think about. I've never brought a man home to him, and I don't intend to start now.

"Are you going to say anything?" His voice is wobbly. I know it took everything in him to ask me that one thing. To push aside his grouchy exterior and be vulnerable for even a moment.

"I'm sorry," I begin. Who knew turning a guy down would be so difficult? "I ca—" The words die on my lips. Nathan walks through the doors and toward the bar. There's no way he won't see me. "Oh shit."

4

carlos

I'M NOT ENTIRELY sure what just happened. A moment ago, she was about to turn me down...I think. Actually, I'm sure she was going to say no. I know rejection when I see it. But something caught her attention. From the way her skin pales, it's not a good thing. "Caroline?"

Her eyes are wide when she turns in my direction. "He can't see me here." Then her cheeks turn a bright red. "Though that explains why he didn't bother to pick up his son. Selfish son of a bitch."

She's angry now. I don't know what to do. Of all my time keeping drama out of the bar, I have a feeling I'm about to be thrown into it. Whether I like it or not. "Who are you talking about?"

"Him," Caroline nods in the direction of the couple walking toward the bar. Her movement is small, but it's just enough to catch the man's attention. "Damn it. He's coming this way."

She's not wrong. The man looks to be a few years younger

than me. There's something about him that makes me not like him immediately. The woman with him looks like she's barely out of high school. She's confused while he looks like a predator who has just latched onto his prey. "Should I go?"

Her hand flies to my leg and squeezes. I guess that's a no. I look toward the bar to see what the idiots who put me up to this are doing. Both Eric and Angie are pouring drinks, but their eyes are glued to this table. Weighing whether or not they should intervene or keep their distance. I give a quick shake of my head and they nod. Even though they are a pain in the ass, I know I can count on them to understand what I need. Too bad, they'll never get the joy of seeing me go on a date with the woman beside me.

Caroline's grip on my leg tightens as the couple approaches the table. She doesn't say anything, only waits. Her entire body is tense beside me, and I wish I knew the back-story. Why does this man make her so rigid?

"Hello, Caroline." The man's voice is smooth and confident as he looks down on us. "Fancy seeing you here."

"I could say the same," she forces the words between gritted teeth.

He smirks and pulls the woman beside him closer. "Don't be upset. I had this dinner meeting set up for weeks. I'm sure David understands."

"Huh. A meeting?" I don't miss the way she surveys both of them. The closeness between them or the way his hand is placed firmly on the woman's hip. It definitely doesn't look like a dinner meeting to him. It looks like a date. I'm also guessing this is her son's father.

"Yes." He takes a step closer to the table. "And who is this?"

I'm not a fan of how he asks the question. Why does it matter who I am? I open my mouth to answer, but Caroline's nails dig into my leg. Damn this woman has a grip. Even though I know nothing will ever happen between us, I can't help but envision her nails digging into my back. Her underneath me. I've only witnessed this woman from afar, and I already long to have her in my bed.

"This is Carlos," she's quiet for one, two, three seconds and adds, "my boyfriend."

The man's jaw drops. My face probably looks exactly the same. I literally asked her out minutes ago. Rejection on her tongue before she got distracted, and now she's claiming I'm her boyfriend. What the fuck just happened?

"I didn't know you were dating."

"Well, I am." Her teeth are gritted as the words slip through them. He's putting her on edge, and that is not okay. I need to do something to diffuse the situation. Or, at least, get the attention off her. If only for a few moments.

I stand and put my hand out in his direction. "It's nice to meet you…" I let the words trail off to see if he'll supply them.

"Nathan." He grips my hand much harder than necessary to shake it.

I pull my hand back, but I don't sit down. I've served guys like him more times than I can count. They think they are better than you for whatever reason, but really, they're douchebags who get their jollies off on making people feel small. I will not give him the opportunity by allowing him to look down on me.

"If you don't mind, Caroline and I would like to get back to our date." I motion to the woman whose night I most surely ruined when I spilled the drink. Happy to save the day for her, even if it's taken me by shock. "And I'm sure you're late for your dinner meeting."

His body is rigid and I know I've hit a nerve. Good. He made Caroline feel like shit and I can't stand by that. I don't care that she's using me to be her pretend boyfriend. Nathan glares at me before stalking away, dragging his date behind him. I kind of feel sorry for her. The night probably isn't going to end the way she planned.

"Are you okay?" I sit down again. But Caroline eyes are fixed on his retreating figure. "Caroline?"

"What?"

"I asked if you were okay."

She shakes her head. It's not an answer. More of a way to loosen her body up after the interaction we just had. I want to talk to her about it, but she doesn't give me the chance. "I need to go."

"I'm not sure you should be driving right now." Besides what will that dirt bag think if he sees her rush out of the bar. "Stay and collect yourself. I'll bring you a bottle of water."

"Okay."

I get up and head to the bar. Eric is there and I know he wants to know what happened, but I can't tell him. Not right now. "Toss me a bottle of water, please."

"You got it, Boss." He bends down to the fridge, grabs the water and hands it to me. "I expect a full report when you get back."

Turning toward the table, I shake my head. She's gone. I rush over to see if she left a note. Anything. But nope. Just a few bills on the table to pay for her drinks and the book I ruined earlier. There's no sign of her at all.

As frustrating as the whole night has been, I find a tiny bit of comfort. I pick up the book and carry it with me to the bar. She has to come back for it at some point.

* * *

Caroline left two hours ago and I'm still unsure what to make of things. Telling her ex I was her boyfriend was definitely a shock. But I'd do it time and time again. Even if it isn't real.

Anything to see the stress leave her body. To keep her from feeling small.

"So, are you going to tell us what happened when you were over there?" Eric is like a dog with a bone. He refuses to let it go. Angie is just as bad. She's practically bouncing on her toes in anticipation.

"Not right now." I pour another drink. "We still have customers and a job to do."

"You're no fun." Angie sticks out her tongue. Considering she's around my age, she can be so childish at times.

"She's right." Eric pushes past me to grab a bottle of liquor. There's a crowd around the bar and we don't have to sit here and chit chat.

The music coming through the speakers is just loud enough to drown out my thoughts. To keep me from wondering what everything means with Caroline. Now the focus is on serving our customers, and keeping them happy. As long as they are content, we don't get shit from anyone in town and they keep coming back.

Most days I can't believe I stay in this line of work. This isn't the career my parents would have chosen for me. They wanted me to get a degree and land an office job. Something respectable. They needed me to be a good example for my sisters. They didn't need that from me, though. Both of them went on to do their own thing. I chose bartending. It's a job that will pay as long as people are coming to get drinks.

"Hey, Carlos," a voice pulls me out of my thoughts. "Can I get a bloody mary?"

Stella is standing in front of me, waving her hands as if I can't see her. "You know those are morning drinks, right? And tonight's special is wine?"

"I would hope so considering I came up with the themes," she laughs.

I roll my eyes. She may be the best thing that's happened

to the bar since I started working here. "Your wish is my command."

"Don't make it too spicy, though, Audrey will be pissed if it's so hot she can't drink it." Ah, so the drink is for her cousin and not her. Stella is a wine girl through and through. I'll never forget the time I gave her a beer and she spit it out across the bar. Luckily there weren't any customers and we were doing a team building lunch.

"Gotcha. The usual for you, then?"

"Absolutely." She leans against the bar, waiting for me to pour the drinks. "So, I hear you finally talked to Reaf's sister."

Dear God. Do they have a bet running on what will happen in my love life? Or lack thereof. "Well, it didn't take long to make it to you."

"Don't blame Angie," she holds up her hands in mock surrender, "she's not the one who told me. Eric didn't either. Reaf is the one that spilled the beans. I just happened to be in the room when Johnny was on speaker phone with him."

Of course, he is. I swear he's just as bad as the rest of them. "I'm assuming your cousins also know?"

"Naturally. Don't worry about them. We have much bigger issues on our plate."

"Like what?"

"Tiffany doesn't like the direction I'm going with her wedding, and she's getting hostile."

"She better not try to beat your ass inside this building. I know you're one of the partners, but I will throw all three of you out."

Stella laughs and waves away the statement. "She may be wild, but even she knows to keep her cool in public...most of the time."

Yeah, it's the most of the time that has me worried. I've seen her when she gets mad and it isn't pretty. "Here you go." I hand her the drinks and she rushes back to their table, on the other side of the room. I didn't even notice they came in. Shows how much attention I'm paying.

* * *

Our customers are finally starting to leave. Couples, and groups, make their way to the door after closing out their tabs. It may be a night of fun, but most of these folks still have work in the morning. Another perk of working in a bar...no getting up early. Except I have to tomorrow. I promised my mom I'd help her with her garden, and I don't break promises to her.

Once everyone leaves, we start the cleanup process. Each of us taking a section and working our way toward the breakroom. I'm wiping down the bar when I feel a tap on my shoulder. "You can't blame anything on the crowd now. Tell us what happened."

Eric and Angie lean against the bar, and I don't miss the way a few of the others slow in their cleaning. "What's there to tell? She rejected me."

"Then what was all that with her ex-husband?" Angie asks. She's definitely as bad as Eric.

"I'm not sure," I push my fingers through my hair. It's good to have confirmation on who exactly Nathan is, though. I assumed they were married before with the tension between them, and I can't help but wonder how long ago that happened. "One second she was telling me she couldn't go on a date with me, and the next she was telling that guy I'm her boyfriend."

"She probably freaked out," Eric adds, and Angie nods her agreement.

"Most likely, but I'm sure I'll see her again soon. She left her book."

"She left it? Or, you grabbed it to ensure another meeting?" Angie grins.

"No, she left it." I pick it up from under the counter. "But I'm going to put it in the office desk so nobody tries to give it back to her if I'm not here."

"Good plan." Eric grins and heads to the computer to clock out. "I'm going to head out of here and get some sleep."

"You should go, too," Angie says. "I'll finish up with the rest of the crew."

"Thanks." I'm not sure leaving now would be any help. It'll just give me time to think over every second of the interaction with Caroline.

5

caroline

"WOAH, WHERE'S THE FIRE?" Bryce sits up from where he's lying on the couch. The TV is louder than we normally keep it, and I don't know how he knew I came in. Hell, I don't even know why he's here. He should be out hanging with his friends while he's home from school, not babysitting his little nephew. Though, I won't say it doesn't make me happy to see their relationship stay strong even though we don't live with Mom anymore.

"I'm not sure what you mean." I throw my purse on the couch and haul ass to my bedroom.

"That," he yells from behind me. "Why are you in such a rush? You're home. You know, where you're supposed to relax."

I do my best to slow my steps and attempt acting like I didn't make a complete ass of myself at the bar. That was so unlike me. Not the rejection part. That was going to happen no matter what. Carlos may be hot as hell, and shockingly sweet beneath the hardened shell, but I don't have time for a relationship. Football season starts soon, and David wants to be just like his uncle and play. How am I supposed to juggle work, David's home and sports, and a relationship at the same time. It's too much.

Shutting the door behind me, I lean against it. A few moments. That's all I need to get my composure. To walk out of the room and act like everything is okay. One breath, two, three. Each one slows my heartrate down a fraction. I breathe in and out until my skin is no longer hot and I'm not about to fly off the rails.

One last exhale and I think I'm good. Moving to my dresser I grab the first pair of jammies my hand lands on. I can hear Bryce whisper yelling at the game he was watching when I came in. But I'm not sure where Mom is, and I know they'll want to talk before they head home. Especially if Bryce tells her the state I was in when I got home.

The change of clothes is quick. I throw the clothes I had on, on the floor, not bothering to walk them to the hamper. That can be tomorrow morning's problem. Tonight, I need to get my mom and brother out of my house without them asking too many questions. There's not a snowball's chance in hell it'll happen, but wishful thinking.

I creep down the hallway. If David is asleep, I don't want to wake him up. He's got school tomorrow and being loud will disrupt his whole morning. He's already not a morning person. Yet another reason why I shouldn't date.

Both Mom and Bryce are sitting on the couch when I enter the living room. Mom scrolling on her phone, probably some social media site, and Bryce's focus is one hundred percent on the TV. I think I'm undetected until the floor squeaks beneath my feet. "How was your night out, dear?"

She couldn't just let me sneak past to the kitchen. "It was okay."

"I feel like it was more than okay," Bryce chimes in. I guess he isn't as zoned out as I thought. "Or maybe it wasn't, okay? Otherwise, why would you haul ass through here."

"Language," Mom slaps Bryce's leg. As if she hasn't said ten times worse. She's the most kind and sweetest woman I know. I might be biased, but she has the mouth of a sailor sometimes. I won't even go into how she acts when we're stuck in traffic. She has road rage like no other. "Now, what had you freaking out?"

"Who said I was freaking out?"

Bryce snorts, and Mom shakes her head. "The fact that your voice squeaked tells me everything. Maybe we can help."

"I don't think my baby brother has the life experience to help me."

"Hey!"

"Do not wake David up," I grit through my teeth. "I'll make you stay the night and you can deal with his mood in the morning."

"Yeah," my brother laughs. "Something definitely happened."

"Ugh, fine. Yes, something happened, but I'm going to need wine to say it out loud."

Bryce jumps up from the couch. "I got you." He's back moments later with a bottle and two glasses. When I raise my eyebrows in question, he nods toward mom. "She's driving."

"Why aren't you?"

"She doesn't trust me in her brand-new car." That's fair. I wouldn't trust him either.

Mom grabs a bottle of water from the coffee table as I settle in between them. "So, what happened?"

I give them a quick rundown of the girls canceling on me, and Carlos spilling my drink on my book. Then it dawns on me. I left my fucking book. I was hoping to avoid the bar until next week. My normal time for visiting, but the book is due back at the library on Friday and I need to get it. "After everything was cleaned up, he asked me on a date."

"It's about damn time," Bryce mutters. Mom tries to reach behind me to slap him again, but she can't reach.

"Did you say yes?"

"No," I sputter. "I don't have time to date. I have David."

"You're allowed to have a life outside of your son," Mom pats me knee. She would know. She's been a single mom since Bryce was around eight years old. She dated here and there, but we were always her top priority. And it's not like she went on a ton of dates. I can probably count them on one hand.

"And I do. With my friends. Once a week."

Bryce mutes the TV and gives me his full attention. He must have something to say if he's not paying any attention to the game. "That's fine, but you can have a boyfriend. Have you even dated since Nathan?"

"Nothing serious, but speak of the devil."

"What does that mean?" Mom is on defense. She never cared for him. Not even when we were in high school, but she didn't say anything because I needed to make my own choices. Wherever they led. Even if it was toward a not so fun divorce.

"I ran into him tonight." I wait to see if either of them is going to say something and when they don't, I continue. "He was on a date. I mean, he had a dinner meeting. You know, anything to not spend time with his child on the designated night. Anyway, he zeroed in on me as I was rejecting Carlos."

"Because that isn't awkward," Bryce laughs. "What happened after that?"

This is the part I don't want to say out loud. The one that makes me feel pathetic. Not just because I told him Carlos was my boyfriend. But because I allowed him the power to make me feel small. To feel like even after all this time, I need to impress him. To let him know I'm doing just fine without him. "I may have told him Carlos is my boyfriend."

"I guess that means you kind of have to go on a date with him." Bryce is absolutely zero help.

Picking up my glass of untouched wine, I take a big drink. "That's not what that means. I'm pretty sure he realizes I didn't mean anything by it."

"Either way, I think you should go on a date with him."

Apparently, Mom is also on team Carlos. "I can't mom. The only reason those words slipped out of my mouth is because Nathan was standing there with his condescending frown." Even though he had someone younger than me on his arm, he still took the time out to be a complete ass.

"You can't keep letting him affect you this way." Mom takes my hand in hers. "It's been years. And because of your actions, you need to go up there and apologize to Carlos. He doesn't deserve to be thrown into it."

She's right. Hell, I knew that after I said it. But I panicked and ran. She also doesn't know that I find him attractive. If he had waited to ask me out, maybe when David is much older, I would have said yes without hesitation. "I know, Mom. It was shitty of me to do, but I freaked out."

"It doesn't matter. You're grown, sweetheart. Stop letting that man control your actions," she pauses for a second, "unless, of course, you secretly want Carlos to be your boyfriend."

She's not so wrong on that part. I'll never let her know it, though. "No. I'll clean up my own mess." I stand, hoping it gives the signal I'm ready for them to leave. If I wanted to get crap for what I did, I don't need their help. I'm doing a fine job of that on my own. "I think I'm going to bed. I need to make sure the girls aren't swamped in the morning. Thank y'all for watching David. It really does mean a lot."

"Please," Mom scoffs. "You don't need to thank us. What else would we be doing?"

"Um," Bryce buts in, "she can thank me. Maybe even pay me."

I pick up one of the pillows and throw it at him. It hits him in the face. Target hit. Sibling love at its finest.

"Children." Mom grabs the pillow of out his hand to keep him from launching it right back at me. "Can the both of you act your age?" He sticks his tongue out at me and I give him the finger. "Okay, that's it. You," she points at me, "go to bed. Bryce, in the car."

He grumbles something as he heads toward the door, but I don't catch it. I probably shouldn't get as much joy as I do in picking on him, but he's done the same to me many times over. Even though he's always done his best to help with David, he likes to throw digs when he can. "Goodnight, love y'all."

"Love you, too," they say at the same time as they walk out the door.

Once it's closed behind them, I plop on the couch. What have I gotten myself into? This all could have been avoided if I insisted on helping with the last of the flower arrangements. But no, I let them talk me into taking the time to myself.

There are so many scenarios running through my mind. Going to a different place. Leaving and not giving Nathan the time of day. But no...I'm a glutton for punishment. I let myself be sucked in by the fact he was with someone younger and prettier. Having the time of his life while I'm the one responsible for the upbringing of the child we brought into this world together. I'm not upset about that part. Not in the slightest. David is the bright spot in all my days, even the diffi-cult ones. But he was able to move on so easily while I'm stuck stagnant.

It's fine. I don't need a man in my life. All I need is my son and to focus on building an amazing life for the both of us. We've done okay so far. At least, I think so. He knows he's loved, and even though this isn't the newest house in the world, I've been able to rent Johnny's old house on my own. I even fixed the hole in the kitchen floor. Well, re-fixed it. He was so focused on his wedding; he didn't nail down an entire side. Like I said, perfectly capable of being on our own.

Sitting on the couch isn't going to solve anything, though. I trudge to my room, doing my best to push tonight's problems aside. I can't solve them from home. I'll have to muster up some false bravado tomorrow.

One last look at my phone before I lie down and this whole situation just got more complicated.

There's a single text from Kate's phone.

Kate: Way to go. It's about damn time

I slide my finger across the screen to open the message and respond, but I stop in my tracks. There's a picture of the three of them smiling and giving me a thumbs up. They are going to be so pissed when they realize it's a sham.

6

carlos

"VEN A COMER." I know from years of experience not to argue with my mom. If she tells me to go eat, that's what I'll do. Any other decision is futile and she'll take it as a slight. My grandma was the same way and so are my tias.

"I'll be there in a minute." I need to finish pulling these weeds for her. I'll have to head to work soon and I still have to shower. There's no way in hell I'm going to work looking messy. Especially not when there's a good chance Caroline will be coming in to get her book. She doesn't seem the type to just leave it, even if it is ruined.

"Now, Carlos."

Shit. I pull the last of the weeds and toss them into the garbage can. I've left my mom waiting long enough. If I don't go in now, she'll come out and get me. I yank my gloves off as I walk toward the back door, and toss them on the patio table. My shoes come off next. If I track dirt through the kitchen, she'll make me sweep.

The door swings open and I narrowly miss it hitting me in the face. "I'm here, calm down."

"The food is going to be cold if you go any slower." Mom opens the door wider and I'm kicking myself for not coming in sooner. It smells delicious.

"I know. I just wanted to finish pulling the weeds before I have to leave for work. You still want the best-looking yard in the neighborhood, right?"

"I'm capable of doing it myself."

"I know you are." And she is. She doesn't do well with feeling like she's less than. She's done an amazing job since Dad passed away.

"Then why do you keep coming over here and trying to do everything for me?" Her hands are on her hips and I know she's offended. She only does that when she's about to lay into me.

"Because you're my mom. There isn't anything I wouldn't do for you. It's why I'm here. Even with my sisters. I would do whatever you ask of me." I sit down at the table. I'm not giving her a chance to slap my shoulder. She wouldn't do it hard, but still, it's not exactly something I want to fend off.

"You're a good boy." She walks to where I'm sitting and pinches my cheek like I'm five years old. This is the downside of coming to help her. She treats me like a child. Though, I'll never argue about getting food. I rarely cook since I spend so much time at the bar, and the smell of her food is possibly the best thing ever. Now if only I could talk her into making menudo. She usually only does it for special occasions. I don't know why. It's one of my favorites, and if she truly loved me, she'd make it.

"I'm grown, mom. There's no need to pinch my cheeks."

"Well, I have to do it to someone. Your sisters barely talk to me anymore."

"Because they are teenagers. What teenager wants to hang out with their parents?"

"You did." She's not wrong, for the most part. I was that weird teen that loved hanging out with his parents. Anytime they are around, it's a good time. But it's harder now that Dad is gone. I miss our talks about sports and work. It doesn't help that I can still feel him here in the house, even though it's been years.

"I need to leave soon. The bar needs to be opened up, and Angie won't be in today."

"But you haven't eaten yet."

"I know." All thanks to the path my mind went down in regards to my father. "Is there any way I can get it to go? I promise I'll eat it."

"I guess, mi amor." She sighs and grabs the foil from the cabinet. "I know you love your job, but it'd be nice to see more of you. You don't have to spend every waking moment there."

"I have a feeling that's going to change soon."

"Oh?" Damn it, I've piqued her interest. I should have kept my mouth shut. "Did you meet someone?"

"I don't want to jinx myself, but maybe?" Please don't ask any more questions.

"Can I meet her?" And there we are. The million-dollar question I knew she'd ask. Also, the reason I knew I should have kept my mouth shut, but she was so upset about me leaving. I had to do something.

"Maybe." I hold up my hand to keep her from asking again. "I'm not exactly sure where things stand with her right now. I'm not bringing anyone home to meet you and the family unless I know for sure they are worth it."

"See," she smiles, "a good boy." She pats my cheek before kissing it and giving me a quick hug. "Make sure you eat this before you go to work."

"Promise." The need to tell my dad bye is still there. Even

though it usually took twenty minutes to actually leave because we'd get started on another conversation. One day it won't hurt as badly, right? I turn toward the door and head to my car. I have to return a book to a woman. Assuming she actually comes back for it.

* * *

The bar is unlocked when I get there. I guess Angie opened up after all. When I walk in, Eric is standing behind the bar, checking the inventory. He eyes the wrapped foil in my hands. "Is that for me?"

"No," I groan. "It's breakfast, my mom cooked for me. If I have any left over, you can have it."

"Aw," his head tilts to the side. "That's adorable."

I walk to one of the empty tables and sit down. "Shut up." Unwrapping one of the breakfast burritos, I ask, "Where's Angie?"

"She left already. She was here long enough to unlock the door and let me in." She's more trusting than I am.

Eric's a good kid, but he's new. Well, newish to both the bar and bartending in general. Though I'm impressed he was already going over the inventory without any instruction. There are still times I have to remind Angie to do it, and she owns the place. Not that she works behind the bar all that often. She's usually holed up in the office doing paperwork and looking for vendors that aren't going to screw us on prices. She needs to get with these contractors and see when they are going to be done with this expansion. We need the space sooner rather than later and I'm getting tired of hearing banging on the walls every morning when I'm trying to open up.

"Cool." I take a bite of the burritos and it is happiness wrapped in a tortilla. Eggs with papas. I need to find my mom's secret because mine never turn out like this when I make them. By the time I add the papas to my eggs, they burn and it's just not as tasty.

"Are you sure you're going to eat all those?" Eric is still staring down my food. "It smells delicious." He wipes down the bar and puts a couple of menus out for the lunch crowd while he waits for my response.

Normally, I wouldn't share, but I need to unlock the office and grab Caroline's book. Not to mention finish taking the chairs down from the tables. We open in less than an hour and until a few more people come in, it's our job to get this place going. "Sure."

"Yes," he fist pumps the air and rushes around the bar to sit down at the table with me. "Thank you. I didn't want to be late so I didn't eat breakfast. Then you weren't here and I called Angie. It's been one of those mornings."

"Woah, no need to explain." I don't need his whole life story. I take another bite of my food. And like clockwork, the banging starts in the expansion area. I need to make a point to go talk to them today. It was supposed to be done by now, and yet...here we are.

"You seem like you're in a good mood today. He unwraps the foil. "Does it have anything to do with a certain blonde from last night?"

This is the problem with everyone here being extra friendly. Well, everyone other than me. I'm usually the grumpy one. That's what Angie says, and it's her putting it nicely. I'm sure I have some less than favorable nicknames from some of our employees.

"Maybe working in my mom's yard gave me happy endorphins."

"Yeah, I seriously doubt that," he snorts. He scrunches his nose as one of the power tools comes to life in the dance area. "Hopefully, they are done working before our first customers come in for lunch. I know they've been understanding, but it's getting old."

"Ain't that the truth," I mutter. I finish my burrito and crumble the foil wrapper. "I need to take care of some stuff in the office. If Caroline comes in while I'm back there, come get me. I don't care if anyone else isn't here yet." Standing, I grab my trash and head toward the office. "And pull these chairs off some of these tables, leave the ones in the back for the rest of the staff to do when they come in."

"I see having a possible date hasn't pulled the stick out of your ass." He grumbles.

"I heard that."

"You were supposed to." He yells back. He better be happy I like him, otherwise I'd probably fire him. The fact that he was here early, without being on the schedule, is impressive. As annoying as he can be, he's good at his job. I'll have to keep an eye on him.

My hands fumble in my pocket for the keys and they clang as they hit the floor. I'm second guessing my whole plan to talk to Caroline again. I could easily have one of the other employees give her book back to her. Grabbing the keys, I unlock the door and rush to the desk, unlocking the drawer her book is in. Okay, nobody else has been in here. That's a relief.

I still don't know what I'm going to do about her, though. Last night was a knee jerk reaction. She needed me to play a part and I did. I'd do it again if the situation presented itself. But she left right after everything happened, and nothing feels resolved. What if she comes in and blames me for taking advantage of the situation? She's not completely wrong, but someone had to put that asshole in his place, and I'm happy it was me. Though, she could have handled it on her own. She threw me in the middle. I should be upset, or mad. Something. I asked her out and she was preparing to let me down gently. Then to be thrown in the middle of whatever is going on between them and the whiplash that caused.

I hear more people talking in the bar area, and glance at the clock. Good, not time to open yet. It's just the rest of the morning crew. I have a bit to wrap my head around everything. The hope and possibilities I felt not even an hour ago is slipping away into fear. I know her friends keep trying to hook us up, not unlike my fellow employees. But what if she thinks I'm not good enough for her. Or, even worse, agrees to go on a date with me because she pities me.

That's it. I'm not going to give her the book myself. I grab it from the drawer and walk toward the door. I didn't pay attention to the cover before, but it's definitely not something I assumed she'd read. I had her pegged as a thriller reader, but this...it has a woman on the cover in a crouch with a red dress. She looks dangerous, but also independent. I glance over the title, *Soulbound*. From the words on the cover, it looks like a witch book, and now I'm intrigued. I usually read apocalyptic books, but maybe reading this will help me learn a bit more about her. I make a mental note to stop by the bookstore at some point this week.

As much as I want to talk to her, I can't. Not with all the doubts ringing through my head. I walk out of the office and down the hall, prepared to have Eric pass along the book. But stop in my tracks when I get to the bar. We're not open yet, but there she is standing just inside the door, looking around the room until her eyes land on me.

7

caroline

OH SHIT, he's here. All the bravado I felt after talking to the girls has vanished. I must have left it in the car because this is terrifying. They think I should give him a chance and go out on a date. I'm just not ready for that. You'd think after all these years I would be. But the thought of going out with someone is enough to give me hives.

My entire goal is to come in here, talk to him and apologize for throwing him under the bus last night. Oh, and my book. I can't forget that because I'm going to need that to return to the library...eventually. Tessa Adams is one of my favorite authors. At this point I've checked out this book more times than I can count, and I should probably just buy it.

But the apology is the main goal. And now that I see him on the other side of the room, I want nothing more than to turn around, open the door and walk out of this bar. Possibly never come here again. Who knows I may ask the girls if we can go someplace else for our Wednesday night romps. I mean the winery isn't that far away. It's actually closer to me. They'll never agree, though. They like the vibe. And I don't blame them. I do, too. It's one of the reasons I like coming here. Well, other than ogling the bartender. Not that he needs to know that.

He takes a few steps into the room and instinctively I take one back. No, not forward like any sane person would because I am terrified. I'm sure I look like an idiot I almost make a dash for the door but before I can turn around, I hear a soft click behind me. Glancing over my shoulder, I notice one of the employees has locked the door. Which would be creepy under other circumstances but they had to unlock it for me to even come in. I should have waited to come during business hours. At least then Carlos could have been busy and I wouldn't be standing here acting like I don't know how to move. Or form sentences.

Okay, Caroline. Time to put on your big girl panties and deal with the situation. All you have to do is get your book and apologize. That's it. So, what if you run into Nathan and he has to ask you where your boyfriend is. You can tell him you broke up. People do it every day. Hell, he did it to me. But from the whispers of the bartender, and the other employees, that's not going to be so easy. And if they are talking about it, I'm sure other people in town are talking about it. How in the world do I get myself into these situations?

Maybe I can propose an arrangement of sorts, like he just tell people he's my boyfriend but not actually do anything about it. Soon the choice is taken out of my hands. Because while I've been in my head, he's closed the distance between us. His eyes glance everywhere in the room except at me. I have a feeling he's just as nervous as I am. Or he's pissed about last night. At this point, it could go either way. With my luck it's the latter.

"Hey," I say and force a smile on my face. I don't want him to think I'm here against my will even though technically I am.

If my friends found out I didn't stop by, they would drag me here themselves and watch over me until they made sure I talked to Carlos. Plus, the guilt trip my mom put me through. Avoidance has never been something she's practiced. And then she had me. The master of avoiding confrontation, even if it's of my own making.

"Hey," he answers, and runs a hand through his hair. I can't help but notice the muscle straining against his shirt. He's too attractive for his own good, no matter how awkward this is. It's like we're two teenagers at a school dance circling around each other. "You, uh, left this here last night." He shoves the book in front of my face.

"Yeah, I know. I'm sorry. I got flustered and left." I mean clearly. It wasn't exactly my finest moment. A quick look around the bar, and I'm mortified. Everyone is acting like they are working, but their attention is one hundred percent focused on us. Especially the other bartender. If I didn't know any better, I would think they are as invested as my friends are.

"I know," he chuckles. "I went to go get you a bottle of water. When I turned around, you were gone."

"I'm sorry about that," I grimace. "And, I'm sorry if I made you uncomfortable by telling my ex-husband you were my boyfriend. That was insensitive of me." The sentence comes out in a rush, the words jumbled together. It'll be a miracle if he can understand anything I just said.

"It's okay, Caroline." He moves his hand as if he's going to touch my shoulder, but quickly pulls it away. "I understand, and if you ever need my help like that again. I can do it."

Whoa, talk about unexpected. Although I guess I can't really blame him, considering he was also going to ask me out on a date last night. So, I get it, sort of. Even if I'm not entirely sure why he wanted to do that anyway. Surely, he knows I have a kid, and if he doesn't...well, that is going to be a rude awaken-ing. Not many guys want to start anything with a woman who comes with baggage, even if they say they are okay with it. I tried that once with a guy who was *cool* with me having a child and got burned. It's why I've only ever focused my attention on me and David. He gets me through every day, and I don't have to worry I'm going to let him down with any choices I may make.

"Why are you so nice?" Nobody is genuinely that good or sweet. It seems mythical.

He shrugs, and shoves his hands in his pockets. "I don't know. I just think about my sisters. I wouldn't want anyone making them feel like they are less than they are. It's shitty."

Huh. That actually makes sense. Also, good to know he has sisters. "How old are they?"

"Teenagers," he shivers. "I don't remember being quite so extra when I was their age."

"You also weren't a teenage girl."

"What does that mean?" He scratches his head.

"Nothing you'll ever have to worry about." I smirk. I don't think any guy will ever understand everything a teenage girl goes through. Or the double standards they are held to. Not that boys don't go through changes of their own. It's just...not the same.

He pulls two chairs out from under one of the tables, and motions for me to sit. "I guess I should be happy about that."

"Yeah, probably." I sit down opposite him. I should leave, but things are less awkward now. It's not like he's trying to hit on me or anything. We're only talking. Like normal people. "I really am sorry, though. It wasn't right for me to do that. Especially after you asked me out and I was trying to tell you no."

"Why is that?" The question isn't angry. It's filled with curiosity.

"What?" Playing dumb definitely isn't smart, but it'll buy me some time.

"You know exactly what I mean." He leans back in the

chair and puts his arm on the table. To anyone watching, he seems relaxed. But I can see the hurt behind his eyes, and I feel like shit for being the one to put it there. "Why were you going to reject me?"

"It's not a good idea."

"For whom? You or me?"

I sit up straighter to hide the jab he unintentionally threw at me. "Both of us. I have a child to care for. Between work and him, I don't have a ton of free time for dating."

He nods. I think he's agreeing with me, but he opens his mouth and makes his counter argument. "Except you clearly have a sitter of some sort. You're here every week. And I have a feeling your ex-husband flakes on his son...a lot."

Damn, he's not pulling his punches. "I do, but it's a regular thing."

"I see." With his free hand, he rubs the bottom of his jaw. I try not to let that distract me. But his jawline is to die for. Also, I never realized how sexy that feature can be. "What if I made a proposal?"

This isn't going the way I expected at all. Hell, I should already be gone. I'm sure the girls are wondering why I haven't shown up at the flower shop yet. I can't let him know how nervous he makes me, though. "Such as?"

"Clearly you don't want your ex to know that you lied about having a boyfriend." I open my mouth to argue, but he holds his hands up to stop me. "I also know you don't actually want a relationship."

"So, we're on the same page. If he comes into the bar when I'm here, we'll pret..."

"You know this town as well as I do. I mean look around us," he motions to the room. Every single employee is watching us, and when they notice my attention, they snap back to working. Shit. "If my co-workers are eavesdropping, and have been, you know deep down others were listening last night. The old ladies here love nothing more than gossip, and I know that for a fact. I help serve them during brunch."

"What are you suggesting?" I knew last night was going to bite me in the ass, and here we are.

"We continue to fake date." He leans toward me with one elbow on the table. He's less than a foot away from me, and despite my better sense, I want to close the distance. Calm down, Caroline. "It'll keep your ex from bothering you if he shows up, and you won't have to worry about anyone telling him it was a lie."

Hmmm, that can't be all. "What's in it for you? Don't get me wrong, it's sweet. But people aren't that nice without wanting something in return."

He points his thumb over his shoulder. "It'll keep these guys off my back, especially Eric. Between him, Angie and Stella, playing matchmaker it'll give me a break from listening to them talk about relationships."

I feel like he's not telling me something. But I get it. It'll also get my friends to leave me alone. He might have a point, even if there are ulterior motives. Little does he know, he won't make his way into my heart. Which I have no doubt is what he's angling for. After the hell I've been through with Nathan, it'll take more than being kind to wedge it open. My phone dings and I pull it out of my pocket.

Kate: Are you coming in today, or are you smooching the bartender?
Caroline: I'm on my way.

I do not have time for their shenanigans right now. "Look, I need to get to work. Do you have pen and paper?"

He pulls a pen out of his pocket and hands it to me. "Sorry, I don't have paper on me."

I glance at the book. It's too damaged to return to the

library. The pages are crinkled from the beer. Turning to the back of the book, I find the list of other books by the author and rip off the bottom corner. I scribble my number and hold it out to him. "Here's my number. Call me and I'll let you know what I decide." I stand and turn toward the door. "But call either late morning or after ten." Confusion passes across his face, but I don't answer his unasked question. "Thanks for giving me back my book, and for last night."

Before he can say anything else, I hurry out the door. I don't know if I'm ready for the barrage of questions from my friends or deciding to accept his proposal. There's a shift in the air, and it's not just the weather.

8

carlos

I DON'T KNOW what's happening in our town. But from the moment we opened until now we have had a rash of customers. And it can't be because kids are in school because they've been in school for a couple of weeks. Unless, of course, now that everybody is in their groove, stay at home moms who are friends can get together and chat.

But now it's nine o'clock at night and I still haven't eaten since this morning. Thank God I brought my mom's food with me this morning so that I would have some kind of sustenance to hold me over. But now that it's getting close to time to call Caroline, my stomach is turning.

Her number is burning a hole in my pocket. I can't tell you how many times I've pulled out the piece of paper, wanting to call her. But knowing she's at work, and then a little later knowing she has her son with her.

She said late at night, but what constitutes late for me is like one or two in the morning. But that's because I work at a bar and I don't have normal hours like most people. For her, though, I don't know if that means nine o'clock, ten o'clock, or midnight. It's a crap shoot. If I call too late, what if she gets mad because she was asleep?

If I call it too early, her son may still be awake and I have a feeling this is something she wants to keep from him. Not that I blame her because he is her child. And who wants to bring some dude that they don't know around their kid? I'm barely trusting of my sister's friends and I'm not their parent. I can't imagine what it would be like if I was bringing a new person around a kid of my own.

This is where it may get tricky fake dating a single mom, but I'm up for the challenge. Especially since I intend to take that fake part out of it.

Even if she is hesitant to consider that aspect. I won't push her too hard, though. I want her to actually like me. "Eric, can you restock the tequila over here? We're running low."

"Sure thing, boss," he grins and heads to the office. One thing I love about this kid is he takes instruction and does what I need him to right then and there. There's no waiting. There's no getting distracted. He does his job, even if he goofs around while he's pouring drinks.

He comes back with a couple of bottles in his arms and is putting them on the shelves behind me. "So, have you called her yet?"

"Of course not." I shake my head and grab a beer for the customer in front of me. I pop the cap off the bottle and hand it to him. He lays down a twenty, and I make a note to put the change in the tip jar. "In case you haven't noticed, we haven't had a lull since we opened, and I'm not trying to call her from behind the bar." I make the change while there isn't anyone directly in front of me. "Number one, she wouldn't be able to hear anything. And number two, it's rude as hell for our customers to see me on the phone."

"No shit," he pats me on the shoulder. "I didn't mean when you're behind the bar. You're allowed to take breaks. Number one, employees have a recommended break time that they're supposed to take. And number two, you're one of the bosses. If you wanted to leave right now, you could."

He's not wrong, but there's no way I would leave these new employees back here with no guidance. Well, they're not brand new. They've been here a couple of months, but they're still new enough that I'm not comfortable leaving them there. Maybe under Eric's supervision, but he still has a bit to go to earn that trust.

"Don't worry, I'll call her when I leave."

"What if she's asleep?" Apparently, I'm not the only one who considers that possibility.

"Then I will leave a message and she can call me back. It's not that hard."

"Or you can text her first and ask her if she's awake." He grabs a glass, a shaker and the liquor needed to make a margarita. "Like normal people do."

"And this is why your generation doesn't have any sort of etiquette. You don't know how to talk to people."

"No," he shakes his head. "We do. We just don't want to."

"I think you may have picked the wrong line of work then."

"When I say *we*, I mean the overall *we* not me. I love talking to people. Thank you."

That I definitely know. Case in point, there is a young lady who's eager to talk his ears off.

Angie walks through the front door and stops at my side of the bar. "Hey, Dylan had a last-minute poker game with the guys. So, I'm coming into work."

"Why?" Eric asks.

She rolls her eyes, "I don't have any hobbies and instead of being bored at home, binge watching Netflix and not leaving the couch for four hours, I would much rather be here."

Makes sense? I wouldn't want to be home and bored either. But I have hobbies.

"Eric and Carlos, you two are free to go/"

"Both of us?" Eric scratches his head.

"I can easily do the same amount of work as you two put together. And you've been here since before the bar opened. You need a break, and I need something to do."

Pfft. I don't know about that. Though she did a great job of running this place on her own with a quarter of the employees we have now before I came along.

"Fine," Eric relents. "But just because you told me to leave from this side of the bar doesn't mean I won't go on the other side of the bar and see if my friends are still around."

"I don't care what you do off the clock, buddy." She must be bored out of her mind if she's willingly coming up here to work.

As much as I was using work as an excuse not to dial up Caroline, being off work means I can actually call her at a decent time. And not when she's likely to be sleeping. I don't want her thinking she gave me her number after I suggested being her fake date, only for me to ghost her. That's not how I do things. And my sisters would kill me.

"Okay, let me finish making this drink, and I guess I'll see you tomorrow."

"Before you go, meet me in the office. Eric, can you cover for just a second longer while I talk to our good friend Carlos? Then you're free to go."

"Sure thing. I can use a few extra tips. It'll help cover whatever I'm drinking when I'm done."

I roll my eyes and make my way to the end of the bar. "Hey, boss," he yells above the crowd. "You better call her."

Good grief. Did he have to announce it to the entire bar

like that? I mean, it takes a lot to embarrass me. But this is one of those moments where it definitely does. The entire bar witnessed my little exchange with Caroline last night. Plus, the conversation we had this morning. How could it not embarrass me to have them know what's going on in my personal life?

Instead of answering, I wave my hand behind over my head so he at least knows I'm acknowledging him. That's all he's getting from me.

Angie's leaning against the desk when I walk in and close the door behind me. I assume she wants this conversation private, or she would have told me out there. "So, you got her number?"

"Is this really what you wanted to talk to me about?" I grumble.

"Yes, and no."

"How can it be both?"

"Yes, because you need to get a life outside this bar. I'm only giving you the sage advice both you and Stella, both gave me. Go out and find happiness."

"The bar makes me happy."

"I know that, but you need to do something else outside of this place."

"Okay." There's no point arguing with her. Outside myself, she might be the most stubborn person I know. "And what was the second thing?"

She takes a deep breath. Shit, this might actually be serious. "I think we should consider moving Eric up to a managerial position."

Oh, okay. At least this bit is actually work related. "This is your big question?"

"Yep. So, what do you think?"

I don't bother sitting in a chair in front of the desk. It implies that I will be here longer than I need to be.

The din of the bar is faint behind the closed door. "I think he is a solid candidate. He gets here before he's supposed to be. He was here before me this morning, as you know. He also takes his job seriously."

"Excellent." She taps her fingers together the way the villain on one of those cartoons does. "That's exactly what I was thinking and why I wanted to talk to you about it."

"I'm not saying make him a manager right this second. But I think it's something we should look into. I know he hasn't been here long, but he's probably the best bartender we have aside from us."

"He is your opposite in every way. You're grumpy and broody and he's happy and outgoing."

"I'm not broody."

"Yes, you are. You're making the broody face right now." She tilts her head to the side. "But that may change from what some of the other employees were texting me this morning. It looked like you were downright joyful."

Jesus. Is this what I have to look forward to? All of my coworkers spying on me and reporting to her like I'm some kind of project they are working on together. There's no reason my personal life should be any of their concern, and that remark doesn't demand an answer. I know that's what she's looking for. "Can I go now?"

"I'm not holding you hostage, dummy. Last time I checked, you own a share of this bar, too. You're free to leave whenever you want. I'm sure you have more important things to do."

"Not that it's any of your business, but yes, I do."

"It better be calling Caroline."

This is why I didn't really need to tell my mom about the prospect of a girlfriend. The people around here seem to think they need to parent me. I stalk to the door and wave goodbye.

If I open my mouth again, she'll just have something else to say. Whether or not it's helpful.

With the door open, music fills the space, and I head into it. Now the biggest question of the night is do I call her from the car, or wait until I get home?

9

caroline

"MOMMY?" David walks down the hallway, and I set down my glass of wine. "I'm thirsty."

He hands me the glass he keeps in his room and it's half full. "You still have water in here, honey."

"But it's not cold anymore." Of course, it isn't. He was supposed to be asleep an hour ago. We don't do hard bed times, but he knows when he goes to bed, he doesn't need to get up again unless he has to go to the restroom. The only thing I can figure is he feels whatever energy I'm putting out there, thanks to Carlos.

"Okay, I'll get you some more. Go to the restroom while you're waiting, then go to your room." It's best to get that out of the way, otherwise he'll come out of his room again. I don't have the energy for that tonight if I'm being honest with myself.

He walks back down the hallway, and I hear the bathroom door close. Getting up, I head to the kitchen and pour the warm water into the sink.

Instead of refilling this glass, I get one of my metal tumblers out of the cabinet. That should keep him from getting out of bed with this excuse again. I turn toward the fridge and push the cup against the dispenser, filling it with ice, then water.

This will hopefully put him down for the night. What if Carlos calls before he goes to bed? I should have gotten his number so I could call him when it's appropriate. But, no, I was ridiculous and didn't think that far ahead. I had to get to work, and that was the fastest way to get him my information.

"Are you coming?" David's tired voice pulls me out of my thoughts.

"Yes, I'll be right there." I pull my phone out of my pocket and toss it on the couch. It's nights like these, when I'm anxious about other things, that it'd be so much easier to share the responsibility. My mom's help is great, but it's not the same as having someone here all the time.

He's sitting on the edge of his bed when I walk into his room. I didn't even hear him come out of the restroom. He reaches for the cup. "Thank you."

"You're welcome." I wait for him to take a drink. He sets the cup on his nightstand and pushes the blankets over to lie down. I pull them over him. "You need to go to sleep now. You have school tomorrow."

"Can you tuck me in like a burrito?"

"Absolutely." I push the blanket underneath him until he's swaddled. I thought kids grew out of that when they were babies, but I think I get it. It's a sense of comfort. The same way my weighted blanket makes me feel secure. Leaning down, I give him a quick peck on the forehead. "Goodnight. I love you."

"I love you to the ends of the universe," he responds. A part of me wonders if he'll outgrow this, and I hope like hell he'll keep this sweetness as he gets older.

The nightlight by his door, and the hall light, are the only things lighting my path out of his room. I close the door, but leave it a few inches ajar.

I turn off the hall light as I head back to the living room. Plopping on the couch, I take a drink of my now warm wine, and press play on the remote. Luckily, David didn't come all the way in here because where it was paused isn't exactly child appropriate. Vampire shows are my go-to when I need a pick me up from a long day.

My phone lights up and vibrates where I threw it. There's only one person it could be. The thought of not answering passes through my mind for a split second. Am I really ready to take this step with someone? Even if it is fake. If I don't, the girls are going to want to know what happened, and I'll be forced to tell them the truth.

Without a second thought, I pick up the phone and answer it. "Hello?"

"Hi, Caroline?" I hear music in the background. I can't tell what it is, and I hope he isn't calling from the bar.

"Who else would it be?" Smart ass defense mode activated.

"You're right," his voice wobbles, and now I feel like crap. The music stops and I hear a door close. "I'm sorry. Is it too late to call?"

I glance at the clock and it's a little past ten. For most people, it's not. But I usually go to bed shortly after David. Between work and helping David with his homework, I'm wiped. "Nope. I actually just got my son back to bed."

"Let me guess...he needed to go to the bathroom?"

"Close," I laugh. "His water got warm, and he wanted a drink."

"Solid reason." Another door opens, then closes, and something clatters on his end of the phone.

"Is everything okay over there?"

"Yes, why do you ask?"

"I keep hearing noises." That reminds me I need to pause my show. Otherwise, he might hear vampires having sex in the background.

"Sorry, I just got home."

"It's okay. I thought you might still be at work."

"Not at all. Angie let Eric and I go early tonight." He brought up Angie, and she's common ground between us. Well, other than the bar. She's someone we both know.

"Why?"

"She was bored and her boyfriend is playing poker."

"That actually makes sense. If there's anyone who would rather work than be bored, it's her." Jesus, this conversation is as riveting as talking about the weather.

"Pretty much. I'm surprised I haven't caught her sleeping up there. She still lives for the bar, but slightly less since Dylan's been in the picture."

That brings up something I've been wondering about. "So, how is this supposed to work? The whole fake dating thing. Because you're at the bar as much as she is. How are you going to have time?"

"Honestly," he clears his throat. "I haven't really thought that far ahead. I was going to ask if you wanted to meet for breakfast in the morning to go over boundaries."

His voice sounds deeper over the phone and I could easily get lost in it.

"I still haven't agreed to it."

He chuckles and I swear my heart skips a beat. Calm down, body. This is all pretend. "Well, you answered the phone, so I'm taking that as a good sign."

I guess he has a point. He doesn't need to know that I debated picking up the phone. "Why not dinner?" I don't know why I asked that.

"It's Friday night, and it's usually all hands on deck on the weekends. It's our busiest time. But I can see if someone can cover me if that's easiest for you."

"No, you don't have to do that." Duh, Care. You know he works in a bar and weekends are probably going to be off limits. It's not like I could do dinner, anyway. We have a huge wedding we have to set up. I'll be lucky if I'm home by ten. "How early are you talking? I have to take David to school, then I'm free until about eleven."

"So, is that a yes to keeping up the ruse?"

Rolling my eyes, as if he can see me, I sigh. "Yes. I don't see a way around it without admitting I'm a liar."

"Good call," he answers. "Does nine work for you?"

I take a few moments to consider it, even though I know damn well that time is perfectly fine. Stubbornness is my superpower. I'm usually done dropping David off by eight at the absolute latest. "Yeah, that works. Where do you want to go?"

"It doesn't matter to me. I'll go wherever. I just need to be at the bar by noon." Huh, he was there earlier than that today. I wonder if they trade off who's going to be there early.

What am I in the mood for? Not fast food, that's for sure. I hear a door squeak open, and that only means one thing. I need to wrap this up quickly. "You know that waffle house across from Brews Clues?"

"Yeah."

"Let's meet there." Footsteps stomp across the floor. I swear this child will never be able to sneak out when he's older unless he works on his step sound. "Sorry, I gotta go. I'll see you in the morning."

"Bye--" I don't give him a chance to say anything else and hang up the phone. "Aren't you supposed to be asleep?" I ask David.

"I can't keep my eyes closed." He does this a lot. I don't know if it's nightmares or just adjusting to the hours I've been keeping. Most days I get home at a decent time, but when there's a big wedding we usually work late into the night. It's possible he could have a bit of separation anxiety. Add in the energy I've been giving off all day, and it's a recipe for disaster.

"You want to sleep with me?" It's the only way he's going to stop getting out of his bed and both of us get some rest.

He nods and walks back down the hall toward my room. "I'll get the bed ready."

This kid breaks my heart sometimes, and I wonder if I've made a huge mistake by agreeing to this entire scheme with Carlos. I grab the remote and turn off the TV, shove my phone in my pocket and turn off the lights behind me as I make my way to the room. He's lying down on the bed with the covers pulled down.

There's a nightlight in my room so I can see to plug my charger into my phone. Plus side, my jammies came on as soon as we finished dinner. I slide into the bed and pull the covers up. "Goodnight, David."

"Can you cuddle me, Mommy?" I wrap my arm around him and pull him to my side. I wait for his breaths to even out before I fall asleep.

* * *

The drop off line for David is winding around the school. Even though I'm here early, there are more cars ahead of me than normal. Rain drops hit my windshield and I realize that's the reason.

Any other day these parents would be rushing to make it before the first bell rings. I didn't even know it was supposed to rain today, but there's no way all these kids are going to get inside the school before the downpour begins.

I shoot a quick glance at David. He has his backpack

already on his back, and is staring out the window. "I guess it's a good thing you wear a hoodie every day."

"Yep," he nods, watching his classmates sprint out of the cars and into the building. "It would be better if it was waterproof, though."

"I'll have to see if I can find you a jacket that is."

"Okay," he shrugs. This kid is unbothered by everything. "But if you don't, it's alright."

We finally inch our way to the drop off area. The clouds above are getting darker, an eerie gray and I hope he makes it inside before the sprinkles turn into actual rain. "Have a good day, buddy. I love you."

"Love you, too. I'll try to stay awake until you get home."

"Don't forget grandma is picking you up from school today. Keep a lookout for her."

"I know." He pushes open the door, closing it with a thud, before dashing down the sidewalk.

I pull out of the school, heading back home to get ready for breakfast with Carlos. Does this count as our first date in the ruse? Or is it just a get to know you situation?

My phone rings. At the same time, a clap of thunder fills the sky, and I jump. Please let me get home before this storm comes at me full speed.

I press the answer button on my phone and Kate's voice comes through the speakers. She doesn't even give me a chance to say hello.

"With this freak storm happening, we're moving the set up to a different time. We'll head over there around three."

"Okay." Damn, this means I won't get home until way later. At this point, I'll ask Mom if David can have a sleepover at her house. There's no use her staying there half the night when I'll be dropping him off with her again in the morning.

"Are you driving?"

"Yeah, I just dropped David off and I'm going home to change before I meet Carlos."

"Wait, back up. You're meeting Carlos?" I didn't mention all the details when I went to work yesterday. Mostly because I didn't know I was going to agree to it until I was on the phone with him.

"Yes, we're having breakfast."

"Okay. Call me on video when you get home. We have to pick the perfect outfit." This is why I didn't want to mention anything.

"I need to go." The rain is coming down harder, and it's hard to focus on derailing the conversation and driving.

"Be careful and don't forget to call me." She hangs up and I continue my drive. With the storm coming in strong, maybe I should cancel. I don't want to get back out in this.

10

carlos

I RUN INTO THE RESTAURANT. My clothes are dripping wet. It wasn't raining in my area when I left the house, but from the water covering the streets, it looks like it's been coming down hard here for a while.

Hopefully Caroline still shows up. Not that I would blame her if she didn't. It's horrible out there. I grab my phone out of my pocket and glance at the screen. No missed calls or messages. That's a good sign.

There's a sign up to seat ourselves. The restaurant isn't full. Most people have gone off to work or back home. Only a few tables have someone occupying them, and I find one in the back where it's relatively deserted.

Before I'm seated, a waitress bustles over. "What can I get you to drink?"

Talk about fast service. Some of our waitstaff could learn a thing or two. Though it would be nice if I could get situated before she came over. "Coffee for now. I'm waiting for someone."

"Okay," she beams, "I'll get that right out."

She bounces off to the counter and makes my coffee. My eyes are on the windows and door, waiting to see if I can spot Caroline get out of her car. A car pulls into one of the parking spots. I've never seen her car, so I can't be sure if it's her.

The door opens, and an umbrella pops out over the top of it.

Damn. I still can't see who it is. They close the door behind them and start walking toward the restaurant. It's not a slow walk either if I had to describe it, it's closer to a jog. And I don't blame whoever it is because the rain is coming down harder than it was when I got here.

Their steps slow as they get to the door and open it. A cool breeze comes in as they close their umbrella outside the door, and shake off some of the water droplets.

Then she turns and my heart stops. She actually came. For a second I was really worried I was going to be stood up. Not only because of the weather, but because she may have come to her senses and realized this is a harebrained idea, and it'll never work.

She looks up and around the restaurant, no doubt looking for me. A few of the patrons glance in her direction, but go back to their meals. I waved my hand in the air to get her attention, and she makes her way to me.

The closer she gets, the more nervous I become. When she's a few steps from the table, I stand up and walk around to the other side, pulling out the chair.

She sets her umbrella against the wall before sitting down and scooting her chair in.

"I'm glad you made it," I say as I sit in my own chair.

"If I'm being honest, I almost didn't come."

"Why?" I genuinely want to know the answer. If she's having second thoughts, I don't want to pressure her into this. Despite the fact I like her, I'm not that type of guy.

The waitress chooses that moment to show back up at the table. "Here's your coffee," she turns toward Caroline, "and what can I get you to drink?"

"Coffee for me too, please."

"You got it." She hands us two laminated sheets of paper. "Here are the menus and I will take your order when I come back, or whenever you're ready."

"Thank you." I reach for the cream and sugar, pulling the whole container in front of me.

Instead of answering my previous question, Caroline watches me fix my coffee. And gapes in horror. "I'm pretty sure that's not coffee anymore."

She may be right. It is definitely more cream and sugar than coffee. But I can't drink it if I can still taste the coffee. It's just not good. At least, in my opinion. But who am I to argue? "Don't knock it 'til you try it."

"I'm not knocking it. Well, I'm trying not to judge your coffee choices. I know everybody has their preferences, but I'm pretty sure your dentist is going to hate you with all that sugar."

"Probably if I went and saw one."

Another gasp, "That's just not even right. How do you go so long without seeing one?"

Just the mention of a dentist sends a shiver down my spine. "I had a really bad experience with one when I was a kid. It's not my favorite place to visit."

"That's fair." The waitress comes back with her coffee and sets it in front of her.

"Here you go, what can I get y'all to eat?" She holds her notepad out and has a small pen in her hand.

"I'll have the waffles and bacon." Caroline answers without hesitation.

That actually sounds pretty good. "I'll have the same." I hand my menu to the server and she leaves us alone once again.

"So, are you still on board with our little agreement?"

She fidgets in her seat and takes off her jacket. I'm surprised she still has it on. "Yes," her voice is barely above a whisper.

"Caroline, if it's something you aren't comfortable with, we don't have to go through it. The chatter will die down with my coworkers one day. And, maybe y'all can move your girl's night out to a different night to avoid your ex."

I can see her work through every one of my suggestions. "No, Wednesday nights have become a tradition. Nathan very rarely shows up to pick up David, and now my son looks forward to those nights with his grandma." She chews her bottom lip, and I wish I could do something to keep her from worrying about all this. "And now that Nathan knows I frequent the bar, and you work there...he's going to make it a point to show up as often as he can."

"Why would he do that?" I run a hand down my face. "Is your divorce fresh?" I can't believe I didn't think to ask yesterday morning before I devised this plan.

"Oh, God no. We've been over for a long time. David was a baby, and he's seven now."

It takes everything in me not to react. Seven years, and he still has this much power over her. I don't understand wanting to be that domineering over someone you left. Maybe through all this, she'll open up to me more. Tell me why she still cares what he thinks. "That's really good to know."

"Why?"

"Self-preservation? I just didn't want to get between a messy divorce, or something that would put you at more risk."

"I'm not scared of him," she scoffs. "I just don't like the way he makes me feel like shit when I'm the one raising our son on my own, as if I'm not allowed to have a life."

The frustration comes out loud and clear. So loud that a few people turn their heads toward us. I wave them away and admire the strength of the woman sitting in front of me. I'm still nervous about dating a single mom. But the fact that she didn't even want me to call her while her son was awake speaks volumes about how protective she is over him.

"I can understand that." Not completely, but for the most part. Mom is now a single parent to two teenage girls and as much as I try to help with the house stuff...I don't really try to act like a father to my sisters. I'm their brother, and I try to keep the line there.

Caroline leans back in her chair and gives me a quick once over. "So, what's your story?"

That's something I've never been asked, and I'm not sure whether I want to open up. At least, not all the way. "There isn't much to tell. I have two teenage sisters, my dad passed away a couple of years ago, and I go help my mom out around the house whenever I get a chance."

The waitress comes back with two plates on a tray. She sets one down in front of each of us. "Here you go. Just holler if you need anything else."

"Thanks," Caroline smiles. "And why did you decide to be a bartender?"

"College. I went for one year, and spent more time making drinks for the parties than going to class. It wasn't for me so I went the bartender route."

"At least you knew what you wanted to do with your life." Even though she looks relaxed, I notice the way her body stiffens.

"Do you not know what you want to do with yours? I mean, raising a kid on your own is pretty damn good if you ask me."

"Not really," she sighs while cutting a piece of her waffle, "I was in college for psychology when I got pregnant with David. And then when Nathan left...I had to pause my education and find a job to support him. I reconnected with my friends and they offered me a part time job at the flower shop they were starting up."

"Have you thought about going back?" I take a bite of my own food, and nearly groan with satisfaction. I'll have to come here more often to grab breakfast before work.

"So, how is this going to work between us? We probably need some sort of ground rules." She changes the subject completely, and I think I may have hit a nerve. I won't press, though. There's plenty of time to break down those walls.

"I'm actually not sure. I've never done this before. I mean, we'll obviously have to make it believable. I have a feeling your friends will be able to call bullshit from a mile away if they think it's fake."

"They will," she laughs. "Kate is already hounding me for the dirty details of our breakfast date."

She called this a date. It's promising. "Okay, so you need to tell me your boundaries. You have the lead here."

"What kind of boundaries?"

"Physical." I clear my throat because that came out more like a croak than normal. "Hand holding, hugging, kissing."

Her cheeks turn red and I think I may have caught her off guard. "Oh, um," she tucks a piece of hair behind her ear and takes a bite to buy her some time. "Handholding and hugging is fine. Even an arm around the shoulder, or waist, is okay. Kissing...we'll play that one by ear."

"I can abide by that." It'll be torture on my end, but I'm a big boy and can handle myself. "Any other things you want to cover?"

"No, I think that's it." She taps the table. "Oh, how are dates supposed to work? It's fall wedding season so my weekends stay booked up. And I know you aren't as available on the weekends. Plus, I don't want to be away from David more than I have to be."

"We can keep doing breakfast dates, or even lunch ones

when you can get away. I do think we should sprinkle in a dinner here and there. Nothing over board, but your friends and my coworkers are going to think we're hiding something if we're never seen together at night."

She scrunches up her nose like she's not fond of the last idea, but she nods. "I can do that. We just need to plan far in advance so I can get a sitter."

I finish the last of my food, and set the fork on the plate. "Great. I'll have to find someone to cover for me on those nights as well. A plan is always a good thing."

I glance at my phone and realize we've been here almost two hours. "I should probably head out."

"Me too," she agrees. "I need to go get changed. Lugging flowers to another location isn't always the cleanest."

I wave the waitress over for the check. "How are y'all going to move flowers in this kind of weather?"

"We're hoping it dies down some. It's doable, but it won't be fun or easy. Luckily, the back door of the shop has a small awning and we can back the van up as close as possible." She reaches for her purse and I hope like hell she doesn't think she's paying.

"I've got this." I tell her and wave for her to put her wallet away. "If you need any help text me. I have a feeling the bar is going to be pretty slow, especially if the weather doesn't calm down."

"I can't call you away from your job." She slides her wallet back into her purse. "That isn't within the rules of our agreement. And thank you for breakfast."

"You're welcome." The waitress comes back and I hand her my card. "And it's really not that big of a deal. If anything, having me around may help y'all go faster. The extra set of hands and all."

"I'll let you know." She puts her jacket back on as the waitress hands my card back. I shove it in my wallet and stand.

"Seriously, thank you for breakfast, and for not batting an eye the other night. Next time we get together we can figure out what our exit strategy will be so nobody gets hurt."

Ouch. She's not going to let her shield down easily. "Sounds good." I grab her umbrella from against the wall. "I'll walk you to your car."

"Thanks." She walks ahead of me until we get to the door. I push it open while I put the umbrella outside and pop it open.

"After you," I motion in front of me. I make sure to hold the umbrella over her head and walk behind her. I'm getting soaked but that doesn't matter.

Once we get to her car, she opens the door and slides into the seat. I close the umbrella and hand it over. "Thank you. I'll call you later."

"I'll look forward to it." Rain is hitting me and I'll have to change before I go to work, but I'm fine with that. What kind of gentleman would I be if I didn't get her to her car safely? "Be careful."

"I will." She closes the door, starts her car and drives away. As far as first dates go...that wasn't too bad.

11

caroline

"SO, how did breakfast go this morning?" Kate grabs a rain poncho out of her bag.

"Why are you asking?" There. Answer a question with a question. I wish I understood why they are so invested in my romantic life, or lack thereof.

She sighs as she struggles to unfold the plastic. "Because I want to make sure you aren't self-sabotaging anything before you have a chance to get to know him."

"Here," I hold my hand out. A few years of little league football, and I'm a pro at doing this. I pull the edges and snap it in the air to get the folds to loosen up. "It was fine. He's supposed to call me so we can set up our next date. It's a little tricky with having to get a sitter and all that."

"You could always call him," she says it as if it's obvious and I haven't thought it of myself. "Then your date is on your terms."

Rolling my eyes, I give her back the flimsy piece of plastic. It's hilarious that she thinks that thing is going to keep her dry in this rain, especially when it's coming down sideways. "He knows my situation. Besides, you hounding me about it isn't going to make me do it. You should know this by now, we've only been friends for our entire lives."

"So, if I tell you to do the opposite, you will?" She's never going to give this up.

The back door slams open and we both jump at the outburst. "Whoever ordered the rain needs to send it back," Sam grumbles. "It's not as if we have a wedding to decorate with a pain in the ass bride."

"For some reason, I don't think the powers at large are listening to you."

"Obviously," Sam snorts. She walks further into the storeroom and scrunches up her nose. "Please tell me that isn't what you wore this morning."

I glance down at my yoga pants, oversized shirt, and combat boots. Even if I had, I don't think there's anything wrong with it. "No, not that it matters." Then I take a peek at Kate who is suddenly silent. "Is there anyone that doesn't know about my breakfast date?"

"I'm sure there are people who don't," she squeaks. "I only told Sam and Emily. Oh, and your mom."

"Excuse me, what?" I hadn't planned on telling her just yet. "Why would you do that?"

I can see her swallow the lump in her throat. "Well, she came in here looking for you. I'm sorry, Care, I thought she knew. Otherwise, I wouldn't have said a word."

"She's lying," Emily sing-songs as she rushes into the room. "Sorry, I'm late. There was flooding at the end of my neighborhood and I took the long way around. What did I miss?"

"Well, Kate is telling everyone about me going on a date with Carlos. Sam is bitching about the rain, and I need to call my mom." I walk out of the room and head straight to the office. This is going to be an interesting conversation. I needed to call her anyway, but this isn't a topic I wanted to broach.

Once inside, I close the door and lock it. Blessed silence. Well, except the rain pounding on the roof, and thunder booming in the distance. At least this wedding is inside. If my friends know what is good for them, they'll keep working and won't hover outside the door and listen in on my conversation.

I pull my phone out of my bra and tap my mom's name in the contacts. After a few rings, she finally answers. "Hello?"

"Hey, Mom." I sit in one of the chairs around the circular table. This space isn't big enough for us to each have our own office, and this table was decided on so that we could all equally give our input. Kind of like the round table the knights used, but without the knights. "You have a few?"

"You know I have all the time in the world for my kids," she laughs. "What do you need?"

Brownie points to her for not bringing Carlos up right away. "First, our time to decorate the venue got pushed back a couple of hours because of the rain so I'll be home later than I planned. Can David spend the night with you tonight and I'll pick him up after we're done with the wedding tomorrow?"

"Absolutely," I can hear her grin over the phone line. He's not her only grandchild, but she loves any moments she has with him. "If you need him to, he can stay the whole weekend."

"Why do you say that?"

"Well," she clears her throat, "tell me about your little breakfast this morning. And if you need another night free to go on a date, I'm all for it."

"Oh my god, Mom." I run my hand over my face. "Not you, too."

"What is that supposed to mean?"

Groaning, I stand and pace around the table. "It means all of you are so adamant about me dating him and making it something more than it probably ever will be. We have one date and all of you are basically marching us up the aisle already."

"I most certainly am not." She just switched over to mom voice. "I only want you to be happy and get out and do something for yourself that doesn't revolve around work, or David. It's not healthy."

"I have girl's night every week."

"Okay, and not something that revolves around your friends. I'm not saying you should revolve your life around this new man. All I'm saying is go out, have fun. And then also maybe pick up a hobby. Because, like I said, this isn't healthy."

"You were always there when we were kids after dad left." And, she can't say she wasn't because I remember it distinctly. She rarely went anywhere that didn't include us. I want to provide that same thing for David.

"That is where you're wrong. Do you remember all those nights you stayed the night with your uncle and aunt for the weekend or week? It wasn't always because I was working. Sometimes I had dates. Sometimes I just rented a hotel room for the night so I could have some time to myself. Those things are perfectly okay. And I want you to have those, otherwise you're going to become so burnt out about being a single mom and working without a life."

"You don't know that." My voice comes off like a petulant child, but that's what I feel like right now with her lecturing me. "David already has anxiety issues whenever I don't come home or when I'm home late."

"And that's something both of you need to work through. The amount of stress you're under is something I've been through, and I don't want that for you.

"It took a long time for me to get to a place where I would send you to your aunts and uncles so that I could have some quality time. You have a loving family around you that can provide that for you. Between me, your brothers, and Tonya, they're all willing to do whatever you need at a moment's notice. All you have to do is ask."

And that right there is the hang-up. She knows I hate asking for help. That I hate being reliant on one person. I was completely lost when Nathan left. I didn't have an identity for myself. Everything revolved around him and the baby. I lost *myself* and I never want to be in that position again.

It's also probably why I'm so independent now. Sometimes, to my detriment.

"I'll think about it. Besides I'm sure he works tomorrow."

"Yes, dear. At a bar. Where I'm sure it'll still be open when you're done with the wedding. Just have fun. And if you don't want to go see what he's up to tomorrow night. You can always go see a movie. I've got David. You have nothing to worry about. Besides, your brother has been bugging me to play with him all weekend."

"Why?" I mean, I love my brother and all but he's not exactly the most giving when it comes to relationships outside of himself.

"Because it's football season, and your brother played football in high school, and he wants to help David in any way he can."

Oh, dear God. That could go badly. "Just make sure he doesn't hurt David. I know he has the best intentions but at the same time he's not exactly gentle.

"I know. Believe me. I will be watching them the whole time."

"And make sure he doesn't teach him anything bad. I don't need another version of my brother."

She laughs, "Nobody needs another version of your brother. One is enough. Maybe I can see if Tonya and Reaf have plans. And even if they don't ask them if Leila can come over, then it could be a grandchild grandma sleepover."

"Okay, Mom." There's no arguing with her. She's already made up her mind, and this is the plan. "Make sure he packs for both nights.

"I will. I raised three kids. I think I have this down."

"Okay, well, have David call me before he goes to bed tonight. I'm sure I'll be at the venue setting up, but it'll be nice to hear his voice."

She mumbles something under her breath. And I'm not sure it's something I want to hear, and it's probably good I didn't.

"Love you, Mom. Talk to you later."

"Love you too." Before I say anything else, or backtrack the entire agreement. She hangs up. I swear that woman is going to drive me to drink.

I put the phone back in my pocket, unlock and open the door. To my surprise my friends aren't hovering right outside. They are, however, standing at the edge of the hallway. "I thought y'all were getting the flowers together to load into the van."

"Well," Emily rings her hands together. "We were, but then we heard your voice get louder and decided to see what was going."

"Oh, I see," I nod, as if that's a good reason. "Well, these flowers aren't going to be loaded if we stand here, chit chatting all afternoon."

"Oh my god, you're right." Sam slaps her leg. "Why didn't I think of that?" She rolls her eyes and turns back toward the storeroom.

My friends are as bad as my mom. I'm basically best friends with a version of her. I'm not exactly sure what that says about me.

* * *

Thirty minutes. That's how long it's taken us to get the flowers situated, and not even a quarter of them loaded into the van. It's a slow process for two reasons. One, because the bride has asked us to bring several types of flowers. And two...the rain.

On a normal day, this would have been done by now. But because one of us has to hold an umbrella over the flowers while the other one carefully gets into the van; it's a whole thing and it takes two of us each trip. So, when one duo is loading, the other one is right behind and repeats.

I'm also thrilled I changed because I'm already soaked. The little rain ponchos Kate brought are doing absolutely nothing. We need full on rain suits for this job. But I will not complain. At least I have a job that supports me and David, and puts food on the table. Even if it can be very frustrating.

"Hey Sam," I call to the back. "How many more flowers do we have to load?"

"A lot," she replies. "We may have to take two trips." That's exactly what we need. Any other day, it wouldn't be a problem. Two trips would take no time at all. Today, however, it's a time suck. And I'm wondering if I'm even going to be able to climb into bed tonight.

I'm preparing for the next trip out to the van when a voice comes from the back door. "Anything I can help with?"

My body freezes. Why is he here?

12

carlos

FROM THE WAY Caroline's entire body stiffens, I don't know if coming over here was my best idea.

"Wh-what are you doing here?" Her voice breaks at the beginning, and I feel bad for making her uncomfortable, and putting her on the spot.

Well, this is awkward. Her friends are crowded behind her, doing a bad job of looking unsuspecting while listening in. "I told you I'd come help."

Her cheeks are turning pink. "You said to call you if we needed help. Not that you'd drop by."

Yep. This was a big mistake. The friendliness we showed each other this morning has vanished. Maybe that's only a side of her I'll see when we're alone. Either way, I miss the camaraderie we had only a few hours ago.

"I'm sorry." I point to where my car is parked. "I can leave. We were just dead at the bar and figured Eric could handle the responsibility while I lent a hand."

"No, don't go," one of her friends, I can't remember her

name, calls out as I turn around, "we really could use your help."

Those words stop me. Her friends could be the key to having her open up. To helping not see our arrangement as completely fake.

"Sam," Caroline hisses with her jaw clenched.

"What?" Sam shrugs. "He looks like he has room in his car to put some plants, and we definitely need someone to speed up the process. Even if he just holds the umbrella for us as we walk back and forth."

"You can't just offer up his car." She argues as if I'm not right there, listening in on a conversation that is about me, but obviously doesn't include me.

"But I can," I grin, "I'll do whatever y'all need me to. I only need to be back by eight. I have a feeling once the rain dies down, the bar will be crowded."

"Then why bother helping?" Caroline waves her hands in the air. Why is she so adamant about this?

"Because I want to." I wave her toward me to speak privately. It's raining, but I really need her friends not to over-hear us.

She walks slowly toward me. Each step measured and calculated. Not that I blame her. It is raining after all. "Why do you want to help us so much," she whispers.

Her friends are leaning as far out of the door as possible, without getting wet, and I can see why she's lowered her voice. "Firstly, because I want to. Angie wants to give Eric extra work, and this seemed like a good time. Secondly, if we're going to be dating, people are going to have to see us together."

"You have a point." She pulls the hood of the rain poncho tighter over her head. A moment of indecision flashes through her eyes before she reaches down and slides her hand into mine. "Let the charade begin."

It should bug me she uses charade to describe this. But it

doesn't because right now, that's all this is to her. I'm definitely going to have my work cut out getting her to have actual feelings for me. Well, more than platonic, that is.

I follow her lead, and within seconds we're in the flower shop. Her friends are gaping at us like they can't believe what they're seeing. I'm as shocked by the PDA as they are. Not that it's much, but every touch from her is like a current of electricity through my body.

There are flowers covering every shelf in what I assume is the storage area. How can one wedding require all of this? "Okay," I let out a breath. "Where do you want me to start?"

"Look at him already stepping up to the plate." Kate grins. "You're going to fit in perfectly here."

"It's not like he's going to start working here permanently." Caroline shakes her head. "This is probably a onetime thing."

She's right about that. I won't always be able to lend a helping hand, but if I have the time, I will. "Should we get started?"

Caroline lets go of my hand and points to several white flowers sitting on a shelf. "All of those need to be loaded." Before I grab the first two planters, she puts a hand on my arm. "But you'll need the umbrella. They can't get wet."

"Sure thing." I grab the plants and head toward the door. I set them down beside the door and open the umbrella before picking them back up. Once they are loaded in the van, I head back inside. "You know what y'all need?"

They look at me with confusion. Eyes squinting and noses scrunched up. "What?" Kate finally asks.

"Those umbrella hat things. My dad would use them when it would rain on a job. They aren't cute, but they get the job done."

"That's genius," Kate claps. "I'll look for some once we get these set up at the venue."

We take turns taking the flowers to the van before filling

up the back of my car. My mom has a pretty extensive flower bed and garden, and I don't think I've ever seen this many flowers going to one place.

With both vehicles loaded, we look at our handy work. The rain has died down. It's still there, just not as hard. The ladies head toward the van, and I go to my car prepared to follow them.

Before I even open the door, Kate gasps. "Aren't you going to ride with Carlos?"

Sheer fear is all over Caroline's face. "Oh, um, yeah." She shrugs and heads toward me. "It's habit getting in the van."

"A habit you should break," Sam smiles.

Rushing around the front of the car, I do my best to beat Caroline to the door. She's steps away when I swing it open. She offers me a shy smile as she slides into the car. I hate that they keep putting her on the spot, but it's something we'll have to get used to if we're going to keep this up.

"I'll follow you there." I wave to her friends and get in the car. Once the door is shut, I turn to Caroline. "Are you okay?"

"Yeah." She stares out the window as I pull out behind the van. "This is just going to be a lot harder than I thought it would."

"Why's that?" Whatever comes next is what is going to make or break the whole arrangement.

"I feel bad lying to my friends and family. I mean whatever this is between us isn't real." I wish I could see her reaction, but her friend drives fast and I need to keep my eyes on the road in the rain. It's probably why she's being so candid.

"It's not exactly fake, either." I adjust the wipers to go across the windshield faster. "Even if it's not romantic between us, it's a friendship. And that still counts as a relationship."

"How can you even call this a friendship? Up until two days ago, the most you knew was my drink order."

Ouch. Way to throw a punch to the gut. "That's mostly true. I knew about you, I've admired you from a distance, but I couldn't exactly talk to you with your friends around. Besides, it's a good thing to know what your regular customers like to drink. I'd be a shitty bartender if I didn't."

She snort laughs. "Funnily enough, my friends have been trying to get me to approach you for months."

Now, that's better. That has to mean somewhere under her bravado, she feels some sort of attraction to me. "Why didn't you?"

"For all the reasons I've told you. My son is my focus."

"You know you're allowed to have a life outside of being a mom, right?"

"Gah, now you sound like my mom."

Well, that wasn't the comparison I was hoping for. Nobody wants to be compared to someone's mother. Hell, I don't want to be compared to my own mom. Not that she's bad. It's just weird.

"She sounds like a smart woman."

"She is. But I heard things today that I'm not sure I wanted to. What she said makes sense, but it's hard for me to imagine. Since he was a baby, my life has revolved around him. I've been both his parents a majority of the time. Nathan pops in when he feels like it, but it doesn't happen as often as it should."

I can't imagine what it would feel like to not have a relationship with my dad. Caroline may be one of the strongest women I know having to juggle work and having a small child. "I'm sorry. That has to be hard for you, and David."

"It's definitely not a cake walk." She laughs, but there's no humor in it. "That is why this is going to be harder than I thought. What happens if one of us catches feelings?"

Too late for that. The more she talks, the more she shows vulnerability. The more I like her. She may not be wrong. This could end up a total disaster. But it's one I'm willing to see through. Even if it does end messy.

"I don't think that will be a problem." Lie. "You're pretty adamant, and I'll do my best to respect your boundaries." Another half lie. I'll respect the walls she's put up, but I'm going to try like hell to get her to lower the barriers completely.

She's silent for a few minutes. The steady drops of rain hitting the windshield is the only sound in the car. It's peaceful, and I don't have the urge to fill the silence. She'll talk when she's ready.

The van in front of me slows, and turns down a long driveway. I brake enough to make the turn without sending the flowers all over my car. In the distance I can see a big building that resembles a barn. If we're lucky, they have an awning over the loading zone. We can back straight up to it, and transferring the plants out of our vehicles will be easier than it was loading them.

Sam makes a turn in front of the slide up door, and backs up to it. A small roof hangs over the door and it's high enough that she can back in until the doors are covered. I park beside her and turn off the car.

As I open the door, she places a hand on my arm, "Wait."

"Sure."

She takes a deep breath and lets it out. "Just promise me we can get through this without breaking any rules."

"Promise." And that's the biggest lie I'll ever tell. There's a probability I'm going to break them all. But I'm not about to fuck up this chance to date her.

13

caroline

CARLOS LEFT about an hour after the rain stopped. His employee called freaking out because the bar was filling up, and he didn't have as many hands as he needed. I get it. People were getting off work and wanted to let off some steam. It is a Friday night after all. He was needed at his actual job.

It's just as well, though. He makes me nervous. Not in a bad way, but when he's around I talk more freely than I do to my friends. And I can't deny that I'm attracted to the man. He isn't much taller than me, but you can tell he gets his work out in during work, and he's completely different than my ex-husband. The way he treats me with respect without really knowing me is more than Nathan ever did.

When Carlos is around, I second guess this entire plan we've laid out. Well, I do it when he's not around, too. I know he likes me. He's told me, and he's still willing to play by my rules. But I can't develop feelings for him. It won't work out even if I did. He has late nights and weekends at the bar. My weekends aren't always free either. Especially during wedding season.

And here I am, arranging the last of the flowers around this massive barn. It's not a bad gig, but it gets repetitive. Only a few more to set up, and we're free for the night. Until in the morning when we have to make sure all the flowers are still okay.

"Are y'all almost done?" Kate calls out, breaking me from my jumbled emotions.

I haven't felt like this since I was much younger, and I don't know how to deal with it. I could swing by Mom's house and see what she has to say. But I'm not ready for that discussion. I'll continue on with Carlos and hope like hell neither of us gets hurt.

"Yeah." I answer. "I just need to straighten up this last one and I'm good to go."

"Awesome." I glance over my shoulder and she's fist pumping the air.

Now that everything is in its place, the four us pile into the van. "I'm so ready to get out of these damp clothes and climb into bed." Emily buckles her seat belt.

"You and me both," I laugh. "It's going to be a long day tomorrow."

"Yep," Sam agrees from behind the wheel. "Luckily, we don't have to stay until the reception is over. They want us to take the flowers from the wedding, but said they'd keep the ones for the reception."

Thank God for small favors. I wasn't looking forward to loading all of those back into this thing tomorrow. "That means Mom won't have to keep David overnight tomorrow night."

"Wait a minute," Kate turns around until she can see me over her seat. "You will not go pick him up. I'm sure she has something fun and amazing planned. You deserve a night to rest."

"Or go see Carlos." I can't see Sam's face, but I have a feeling she's lifting her eyebrows up and down.

"He has to work." They do have a point, though. Tonight, and tomorrow, I can curl up on the couch with a book and not have to worry about anything for a bit.

She shrugs, "There's always after work."

I don't bother coming back with a retort. She'll twist my words and use it against me. Instead, I lean my head against the side of the van, and think about everything that's happened today. Soon Carlos and I will need to figure out a date where we're seen.

* * *

We park and get out of the van. All four of us are tired and can barely walk. Setting up this wedding is the biggest we've done since I've been working with them. It makes all the others look tiny in comparison.

"Meet here in the morning?" I ask through a yawn.

"Yep." Sam locks the van and pulls on the handle to make sure it won't open. She does it with her car, too. I'm not sure why, but if it makes her feel better, so be it. "Around eight. It'll give us a chance to check the flowers and do any last minute adjustments."

"Sounds good. Night everyone." Kate waves at us and gets in her car.

"Night," I wave to everyone else and unlock my car door. I slide inside and start the engine, going through all the motions to head home. I wait until my friends are in their vehicles before pulling out of the parking lot. Tomorrow is going to be a long day, and I'm not sure I'm ready for it.

The only problem is, I don't turn down the road that will

take me to the house I rent from Johnny. No, I go straight to the downtown area and pull into the parking lot of Out of the Ashes.

I find a spot and put the car in park, but I don't get out. There isn't a line out the door like there usually is. I guess the rain earlier today still managed to keep some people at home. Which is where I should be heading. Not sitting in the parking lot of the establishment my fake boyfriend works at.

I'm not even sure why I'm here. I think back to when I pulled him into the flower shop this afternoon, and as much as I want to deny it, his hand in mine felt good. How sad is it that the simple touch of his hand in mine, was almost able to reduce me to a puddle of goo. And when we were talking in the car? The way the words flowed and I told him things I've never uttered to anyone else; it was freeing.

There's just something about him, and I can't quite pinpoint what it is. Now, I have to decide if I'm going to leave the lot and actually go home, or go inside. I glance down at my clothes, an oversized sweater and yoga pants. Both are still damp from the rain and most likely sweat. The bar doesn't have a dress code, but I'm sure I look rough.

I have every intention of putting the car in drive and hauling ass home. But my hands don't listen to what my mind is saying. I turn off the car, pull the keys out of the ignition and open the door.

The door is feet away before I remember to lock my car. It's almost like I'm in a daze. I open the door to the bar and walk in. It's nowhere near capacity, which is unusual. The hostess, I think Delilah is her name, isn't anywhere to be found so I find an empty stool at the bar and take a seat.

"Hey, what can I—woah, you look, uh, like you need a drink." The new bartender is standing in front of me. "Are you okay?"

Talk about a winning endorsement about my appearance.

Definitely should have gone home. "Yeah, I'm fine. Just a long day."

"You want your usual?" Damn, even the new guy knows what I order. I'm beginning to think I'm entirely too predictable and maybe what Carlos and I are doing will help shake things up.

"Sure, but water after that. I have an early morning." Leaning my elbows on the table, I cradle my head in my hands. The music coming out of the speakers is loud, but it's mellow. Not the usual club beats that play when we're here on Wednesdays. I thought it would be on Friday night, but I'm guessing the few guests means they can take it down a notch.

Before Eric has a chance to grab my drink, I see a bottle of beer slide into my view. I lift my gaze and Carlos is in front of me a small smile on his face. "I saw you sit down, and figured you might be here for this."

Little does he know, I'm also here for him. Not that he can leave work, but at least I can talk to him for a bit when he's not busy. "Thank you."

"I figured you'd head home after the day you've had."

"Funnily enough, I had every intention of doing just that."

He leans on the bar, "And you magically ended up here?"

"Something like that." I shrug and take a drink of my beer. "Besides, I figured we'd hash out our next date."

He laughs, and it's deep, full, and kind. "I don't think moving flowers counts as a date."

"I was referring to breakfast," I roll my eyes. "But I have an unexpected free night tomorrow night, maybe we could do something when you get off work?"

Where in the world is all this brazenness coming from? I'm never this forward. I can't blame it on the alcohol because I've only taken one drink. Exhaustion. That has to be the cause.

"That sounds good." He glances over toward Eric. "Hey, who is on the schedule for tomorrow night?"

I watch the exchange between the two of them. Eric looks over a piece of paper by the computer. "Me, you, the guy you hired last week, and Angie."

Wow, Angie is working on a weekend. That doesn't happen as often as it used to since she got in a relationship with Dylan. Another drink of my beer and it's halfway down. Okay, so it was more like a gulp.

Carlos taps the table with his fingers, and presses his lips together. "Let me see if I can get out of here early tomorrow. If not, it'll be late." Before I can say anything, someone catches his attention. "I'll be right back."

I watch him take a customer's order and make it. His movements are swift and sure. A part of me wonders if he's as skilled in other areas, and quickly shake the thought from my head. Nope, that's enough of that. It's been a long time, but I barely know this guy. Even if I am attracted to him, I can't be thinking about sex with him. That would be irresponsible, right?

I down the rest of my beer and set the empty bottle on the bar. I grab cash out of my wallet and set it down. The last thing I need is for Carlos to see me blushing because of the thoughts I'm having about him.

Home. That's where I need to be. Sliding out of the barstool, I rush out the door with my name on Carlos's lips following after me.

14

carlos

SHE LEFT. Just like that. In a middle of a conversation. The only thing I can think of is something with her son. It's all I can think about this morning.

"Did you call her?" Eric asks from the other side of the bar.

"I text her last night, but she may have already been in bed." Angie did me a solid and told me to leave after the lunch rush. "I plan on calling her again when I get off work. We didn't finalize our date."

"No offense, man," Eric holds up one hand. The other is holding a broom. "But I'm wondering if she's even into you. I know you like her, but is she worth all this trouble?"

"She has a lot on her mind." We finish cleaning up the area and I flip the sign over to open. Patrick is in the kitchen, preparing his menu, and it smells delicious. "You know you don't have to be here this morning, right? You work until close tonight."

"It's not like I have anything better to do. The more

money I can make, the sooner I can move out of my apartment." He leans against the bar after putting the broom away. "I need my own place."

"Take it from someone who knows, don't burn yourself out."

"Okay, Dad," he rolls his eyes, "up until a couple of days ago, you were doing the same thing."

"Yeah, well. Maybe if I didn't work so much, I wouldn't have waited so long to ask Caroline out."

"You mean, if we hadn't pestered you?"

"Maybe," I shrug. Grabbing the towel off one of the tables, I wipe the bar down one last time. I hear music come over the speakers, at a much lower volume than we play it at night, and I know Eric has taken care of that.

The door opens and I glance up. A part of me really hoped it would be Caroline, but it's not. It's the last person I want to see, and I don't know if I can keep my cool.

Nathan enters the bar with a different girl on his arm. From what Caroline has told me, I don't see how he can hop from girl to girl. He didn't seem very attentive to her and I can't imagine that's changed much.

Eric looks to me when he realizes who it is, and his eyes widen. But he swoops in. "Can I get y'all a table?"

"For two." He doesn't bother looking at Eric, and continues looking at his phone. His friend tugs on his arm, and he shoves the phone in his pocket to follow Eric to a table on the opposite side of the room. But he catches sight of me and stops in his tracks. "Hey, you're Caroline's new boyfriend, right?"

He doesn't deserve an answer, it's none of his business. If he can have whatever relationships he does, she's allowed too as well. But I nod my answer. "I am."

"Huh. I didn't actually believe it when she said y'all were a couple. You both looked like deer caught in headlights." He shakes his head and finally allows his friend to pull him toward the table Eric is already standing at. "I hope you can get her to live a little."

That comment alone makes me want to jump over the bar and regret uttering the words. I can't, though. My name is on the company documents, and I don't want to cause trouble for Angie. My fists clench at my sides, and I take a few deep breaths to calm myself down.

Seeing him size me up from his table, while parading different women in here, isn't making it easy. "Hey, Boss," Eric whispers from the front of the bar. "Are you okay?"

Releasing my fists, I nod. "Yeah. Can you handle up here? I need to go to the office before I do something I'll regret."

"Sure thing. Delilah should be in soon, and she can help with any other customers who come in."

"Thanks." With every passing day this kid works here, he's definitely earning that assistant manager title. His ability to read situations on the fly is exactly what we need.

My steps are slow as I walk to the office. I don't want that douche thinking I'm running away. No, I have a new plan. I'll show Caroline that I'm nothing like that arrogant ass.

* * *

Work flew by after that little incident. I managed to stay in the office and away from Caroline's jerk of an ex-husband until he left. Eric let me know when the coast was clear. I do feel like a coward for retreating, but it was what was best. As much of an ass as he is, he's still the father of her child. Even if he's not around his son, I'm not going to be that guy that puts more unnecessary strain on their already fragile relationship.

It's already close to five, and I'm pacing my living room. Some movie is on in the background. I don't even know what it is. I just needed a distraction so I wouldn't be checking my phone every five seconds. She still hasn't answered my text from last night. Deep down, I wonder if she's always going to be a flight risk. Hell, I don't even know what I did that would have scared her off.

My phone rings and I stop in my tracks. Turning, I pick it up from the coffee table and don't bother seeing who it is. "Hello."

"Mi Amor, why aren't you at work?" My mom isn't who I was hoping it would be.

"I got off early." I sit on the couch and lean my head back. "Why are you calling if you thought I wasn't going to answer?"

"Can a mother not call her only son?" Slammed with a guilt trip. Before Dad passed away, I'd probably have a snarky answer, but not anymore. Him being gone only signified how much family means, and when one piece is missing...there's a gaping hole in the dynamic.

"Sorry, Mom. How are you?" Most of the time she calls just to talk, but sometimes she needs something. She knows I'll do whatever she asks.

"Bien." She pauses, at least she's good. "Do you want to come to dinner tonight? Both of your sisters will be home at the same time, and it'll be nice to have all my children under one roof."

"I can't tonight, Mom." Please don't ask why, please don't.

"I'm making your favorite...arroz con pollo." Damn. She knows how to entice me.

"Sorry, Mom, tonight isn't a good night. I can come tomorrow night."

"Por que?" Her voice hitches and I know my refusal has hurt her feelings. It would be nice to have a dinner with the family, but tonight isn't the time. Last minute plans are usually how we operate, but I can't do it right now.

"I have a date."

"Bring her."

That is what I was afraid of. After telling her I might be seeing someone, this almost feels like a way for her to meet her before I'm ready. Hell, I don't even know if it will get that far, even though I'd love nothing more than to bring her around my family.

"It's our first date. No offense, but I'm not bringing her to meet my mom and sisters the first time we're supposed to go out."

"Why not? It's going to happen anyway. Might as well get it taken care of." Yep. She definitely contrived this whole dinner on the off chance I'd be seeing Caroline tonight.

"As soon as I know it's not just a few dates, I'll bring her to the house." Please let that be enough for now. I don't like arguing with my mom, and she's making it hard not to be on the defense.

"Fine." She gave in way too easily. "But tomorrow night...dinner."

"Will it still be my favorite?"

"Maybe, pero I don't know if I'll make the tortillas or buy them from the store."

Damn. If I give in for dinner tonight, I also get her home-made tortillas, but if I don't it's the plastic tasting ones. I guess I'll suffer. I don't need my mom grilling her on the first date, technically second. But who's counting?

"Okay, I'll be there. I need to get ready." She doesn't know that I haven't been able to get ahold of Caroline, but she doesn't need to. "Love you."

"Love you, too." She hangs up without saying bye, even though she knows it gets on my nerves.

I really hope Caroline calls soon, otherwise I just lied to my mom and missed out on her tortillas. Standing up, I put my phone in my back pocket. I debate turning the TV off before heading to my room to see what I have to wear, but leave it on for the noise.

The hangers scratch on the rod as I move shirts to find the perfect one. Most of the shirts I own are white or black. There's a button up close to the back. I pull the hanger out and hold it up. I don't even remember the last time I wore this, but a date seems perfect. It's the most dressed up I've been in ages. It needs to be ironed; except I don't own one.

Tossing the hanger on the bed, I walk to the laundry room and throw my shirt in the dryer. My phone rings again, and this time I check who the caller is. I don't want to get bombarded with questions from my family again.

It's Caroline, and I swipe to answer the call. "Hello?" Damn did that sound high pitched? I hope not. Giving the impression I've been waiting by the phone wouldn't be a good thing. Even though that's exactly what I've been doing. I even carried it around while at work, and that's something I never do.

"Hey." Her voice is low and tired. Today must have been as frustrating as last night. "Sorry about last night."

"It's okay. I figured something came up." I don't say anything else, giving her the space to tell me or leave it be.

"Yeah, um, David called and I wanted to tell him good night." The slight hesitation tells me she isn't being completely honest, but I'm not going to push. Not yet, anyway. "Are we still on for a date tonight?"

"Absolutely, what are you in the mood to eat?" There's this nice steak restaurant that opened up not too long ago that I'd love to take her to.

"Actually, can we grab something and hang out at one of our houses? Today was a nightmare and I think a chill night sounds fantastic."

It's not the same as being seen by everyone, but at least her stupid ex knows we're actually together. At least, he seemed to believe it. "Sure. Your house or mine?"

The phone line is silent one, two, three seconds before she finally answers. "Mine? I can send you, my address."

Shock doesn't even begin to explain what I'm feeling. For someone who is so adamant we can't be a real thing, she's letting me into her space. Another chance to get a peek into her life and get to know her better. "Sounds good." Now I don't need that shirt. "Also, how do you like your steak?"

"You don't have to bring anything like that. I'm perfectly fine with fast food."

"Humor me." She sounds like she's had a hard day, and the last thing I want to feed her is a greasy frozen burger from a drive thru.

She laughs softly, and I'm glad she's not going to fight me on this. "Medium or medium well."

"Okay. I can be there in an hour or less."

"Okay. I'll text you, my address. See you in a bit."

"Bye." I press the end button and immediately search the phone number for the restaurant. I hope like hell they do takeout.

A message flashes across the top of my screen with her address, and I swipe it away. I call and place the order. There's one more place I need to swing by before I head to her house. We may be doing dinner in, but that doesn't mean I can't make it special.

15

caroline

I CAN'T BELIEVE I invited him to come to my house. His would have been better. I haven't been home in two days and it's a disaster area. Even though every bone in my body is yelling at me to sit down, I rush through the house grabbing anything and everything sitting out in the open.

The most damning being the clothes I pulled off as soon as I walked in the front door last night. I can't believe I went into Out of the Ashes wearing these. With all the dirty clothes in hand, I open the laundry room door and throw them in the first empty basket I see.

One more sweep through the living room and kitchen. My arms are full of toys and books. Normally, I'd make David clean them up when he gets home, but not with Carlos coming over. I hurry down the hall and put his things on his bed. He can handle that when he gets home. I close the door as I exit the room to keep his mess out of sight.

Walking past my bedroom, I notice all the laundry in there. Not all of it is dirty. There are two baskets of clean laundry I haven't had a chance to get to yet. I pull out the nicest and most comfortable pair of yoga pants I own, a shirt, a pair of socks, and set them on the bed.

Stacking the baskets, I set them on the floor of my closet and close the door. Now for the dirty laundry, I walk through and pick up each item. The laundry basket in the bathroom is full and I set the clothes on top before taking the entire basket to the laundry room. I guess I know what I'm doing tomorrow.

Heading back to my room, I check anything else I may have missed in the hallway. A quick check of David's bathroom, and I breathe a sigh of relief I don't have to clean it. Mom must have taken care of it when she was here the other night watching him.

I glance at the alarm clock and it's been thirty minutes since I pulled in the driveway and got off the phone with Carlos. He'll be here soon and I'm still wearing this itchy dress I put on for the wedding. These need to go. The only plus side of him coming to my house is I'm in my element here, and I can be comfortable.

I pull off the dress and set it on my dresser. It has to be washed separately from everything else and I don't want it to get mixed up. Quickly, I put my comfy clothes on and head to the kitchen. I'm not sure if I left out any wine glasses from last night, and I want to make sure they are put away.

Stopping by the TV, I turn it on and pull up a music app. My cleaning playlist includes music from Panic! At the Disco, and they are the first band that plays. Upbeat tunes make everything go by faster.

The empty bottle of wine sits on the counter and I grab it and put it in the trash. The glass goes in the dishwasher and I make sure there's another bottle of wine in the fridge. I may need it to calm my nerves when Carlos is here.

I still don't understand what it is about him that makes

me nervous. Aside from the fact he's hot, caring, and even though he's agreed this is fake, he seems interested knowing full well I come with a kid and baggage from the past.

The song switches to another upbeat one, and I dance around the kitchen as I put things away and pull down a couple of plates. Regardless of what he gets, it calls for actual plates and not the paper ones David and I usually eat off.

I debate on getting the silverware out, but wait to see what he decides on for dinner. Shaking my ass, I pull down two glasses and turn, dropping both of them to the floor. Glass shards skitter across the wood floor.

"So, you're a Panic fan." Carlos is standing between the kitchen and living room with two bags and a bouquet of flowers in one hand and a pack of my favorite beer in the other.

"Shit." It's the only thing I can think to say. I can't believe he just walked in. Who does that?

I lift my foot to step over the glass, but he sets everything on the table. "Don't move. Where is your broom?"

"In the pantry." I point to the left. He hurries over, opens the door and pulls out the broom and dust pan. His steps are slow as he does his best to avoid the glass and bends down in front of me sweeping up the mess I made. Talk about memorable first dates.

"I didn't mean to scare you." He looks up at me, and his dark brown eyes are full of sincerity. "I knocked and you didn't answer, so I tried the door and it was open."

He looks back down at the task at hand and continues sweeping up the mess. "It's okay." And it is. It's something I think I would have done. Especially if that person was expecting me. But only because my thoughts go to the worst thing that could happen and they may need help. "I didn't realize my music was up that loud, or how much time had passed."

He sets the broom and dustpan on the floor and stands. "At least it was good music." He looks around the floor, inspecting the area. "I think I got it all." I take a step, and he holds his hand up. "But I want to make sure. Do you have a vacuum?" He points toward my feet only protected by a pair of socks. "Don't want you to get cut by a tiny piece."

"Yeah, first door on the right in the hallway. There should be one in there."

He puts both of his hands on my waist and lifts me up on the counter behind me. Not taking any chance of me getting hurt. Not going to lie, it feels nice to have someone care about me this much, and the flutter of butterflies in my stomach is an indication I'm going to fall hard and fast.

He heads to the laundry room to grab the vacuum and I admire the view the entire time. On his way back, he pauses to turn the music down before coming into the kitchen. He unravels the coil and looks for a plug. The only one on this side of the room is right behind me.

Scooting over I point it out, expecting him to hand me the plug to do it for him. But no, he places one hand on the side of me and reaches around me to plug it in. My breath hitches as his hand on the counter brushes against my leg.

If he heard it, he doesn't react. He pulls back and turns back toward the vacuum, turning it on and rolling it over the area both of us were standing in minutes ago. I thought him being in my space would be weird or awkward, but it isn't. Watching him do every day normal things in my home is... different. Not good or bad, but different. Even though whatever this is between us is new, and fake I tell myself again, this feels normal.

The vacuum turns off and he ravels the coil. "I think I got it all."

I could wait for him to lift me off the counter, but I won't. This date has already started off weird. I slide off the counter and bend down to pick up the dustpan. Walking it over to the trash can, I lift the lid and toss the remnants of my glasses inside.

"Thanks for cleaning it up." I stride over to where we were standing and pick up the broom before heading to the pantry and putting them away. "It'll be one hell of a story to tell."

"Like the way you said I was your boyfriend in a crowded bar?" He smirks before taking the vacuum back to the laundry room.

I grab two more glasses from the cabinet and set them on the table. I pick up the bouquet he brought and notice the name of the flower shop. I go to the sink and grab a vase from the cabinet underneath before filling it with water. Placing the flowers inside, I set it on the counter next to sink. "When did you get these? We usually close up early on wedding days."

"I got lucky," he comes into the kitchen and pulls boxes of food out of the bag. "Kate was still there when I pulled up. She tried to give me the flowers you brought back from the wedding, but I figured that's the last thing you wanted to see."

"You'd be correct." I grin and turn to grab some silverware out of the drawer before going back to the table. He definitely did not opt for fast food, and I'm grateful. "This smells delicious."

"It's the new steakhouse in town." Woah, I've heard that place is amazing, and expensive. He shouldn't have sprung for this. Not when I'm literally in my cozy clothes and he cleaned up the mess I made. "I didn't know what sides to get you, so I ordered a salad and potato."

"That's fine with me." I set the silverware down at opposite sides of the table and move the plates to the same spots. He grabs a fork and moves a steak from each box to the plates. Then places a potato on each. Before long we have a full spread in front of us, and I grab the empty bag, setting it next to the fridge.

He pulls two beers out of the case and fills the glasses. He throws the empty bottles in the trash and holds up the box. "Can I put these in the fridge?"

"Absolutely." He sets them in there and waits until I sit down before sitting himself. "Thank you for dinner."

"You're welcome." He grabs the knife and cuts into his steak. "I'm sure it would be better when it's eaten there. Not that I'm complaining. I'm glad I get to see where you live."

"Sorry for the whole staying in thing. The bride of the wedding was...a lot, and I didn't have it in me to go out."

"Understandable. Maybe we could watch a movie when we're done eating."

"I feel like there is a 'Netflix and chill' joke coming," I laugh before taking a bite. "Oh my God," I moan. "This has to be the best steak I've ever eaten."

He mutters something under his breath, but I don't catch it all. All I hear is, "making noises like that and." He takes another bite and nods in appreciation. "I don't even think our cook at the bar could make it taste like this."

"I'm going to tell him you said that. I think his food is delicious."

"I'm not knocking his food. Other than my mom, he cooks the best food I've ever tasted...until now."

I cock my head to the side, thinking about it. "You may be right, but I've also never had one of his steaks."

"You aren't missing much." He takes a drink of his beer and I do the same. "How's David?"

"Huh?" That's a weird question.

"You said he called last night."

"Oh, yeah." I set my fork down. He didn't call. I called him not long after I got home. But there's no way he could know that, right? "He's fine. We still call to tell each other goodnight when he stays over at my mom's."

"He stays up pretty late." There's no judgement from him. It's only an observation.

"Yeah, on the weekends."

"Is that really why you left?" Damn, I was hoping he wouldn't press the issue. It's the only believable thing I could tell him that wasn't the truth. "I'm just trying to understand what this is between us. I know it's a show we're putting on for others, but every time I turn around, you're running out."

I deserve that. Running is what I do when I freak out. "Sorry. I kind of freaked out."

"Why?" He sets his fork down and waits for me to answer.

There's no way of saying this without sounding stupid, so here it goes. "I was watching you work, and it kind of turned me on so I had to leave."

Oh my God, I can't believe I just told him that. From the way his mouth is hanging wide open, I don't think he can either. I'm certain my cheeks are a bright shade of red.

16

carlos

WELL, um, that was unexpected. Now I know why she said she was talking to her son. I also feel bed for pressing the issue. It does boost my ego a bit, though.

"That's good to know."

"This is so mortifying." She covers her face with her hands. "Can we go back to a few minutes ago when you believed my first story?"

Snorting to keep from laughing, I pick up my silverware to eat again. Anything to move on and make things seem normal again. "Consider it done."

Both of us eat in companionable silence. There isn't much to talk about after a confession like that. I take the time to check out the areas of the room I can see. Considering she has a young child; I'm shocked there aren't more toys everywhere. I remember when I was little, I had toys thrown all over the house. Mom was always yelling for me to pick them up before she stepped on another one.

She doesn't have a lot of unneeded things. I'm not sure of

the reason, but it doesn't matter to me. Honestly, it's why I feel comfortable here. I don't have a lot of things either. Being at the bar all the time, I'm never home to enjoy anything. And when I'm not at the bar I'm at my mom's house doing whatever she needs me to do.

"So, what do you want to watch?"

"What?" Caroline finishes her salad and wipes her mouth.

"I thought we were going to watch a movie?"

"Oh, I figured you'd run like hell after what I said. Especially since the conversation died after that." She places her silverware on her plate and stands from the table.

"I didn't think you'd want me to say anything else. That had to have been hard for you. And I decided maybe I should shut up." Hopefully showing my fault in harping on it will ease her mind some.

"It was." She places her dishes in the sink. I grab mine and follow behind her. "But yeah, we can watch a movie."

She starts washing the dishes, and I place a hand on top of hers. "That can wait until later. Let's pick out a movie. What are you in the mood for?"

Eying the dishes in the sink, she relents. "Vampires?"

Not exactly what I would have pegged her to like, but I guess it makes sense after the book she was reading. "Sounds good. I haven't watched a lot of vampire movies so pick one out. I'll be in there in a few seconds."

"Okay," she drawls. She gives me one final look before heading to the living room. I turn toward the sink and make quick work of washing the few dishes we use. "I thought you said that could wait."

"I just didn't want you doing them. After everything you did yesterday and what you've dealt with today, you deserve the break."

I glance over my shoulder to see what she's doing, and

she's smiling. An honest one that isn't forced or self-deprecating. "Thanks."

The music stops and I hear the clicks as she searches for a movie with the remote. I grab two beers out of the fridge and pop the tops off before joining her on the couch. I hand her one of the bottles. "What is this?"

She gasps, and I wonder if she's choking on the beer, I just gave her. "You've never seen this? It's not exactly new."

"Um, no." Clearly, or I wouldn't have asked. "I'm going to assume it has vampires."

"And werewolves."

"This isn't that movie all the teenage girls were obsessed with, is it?" Please say no. I don't know if I can handle sparkly monsters with a straight face.

"No. It's better. She proceeds to tell me the basic plot of the movie.

"What? A vampire and werewolf being together? I thought they were enemies."

She shakes her head and rolls her eyes. "Just watch the movie. You'll like it."

"Okay." I'm not so sure. Maybe I'll like it, though. Either way, it means being close to her and I'll take it.

Caroline presses play and leans back, propping her feet on the coffee table in front of us. I'm not comfortable putting my feet on her table, so I settle in next to her.

Her head is on my shoulder within minutes and I can't help but wonder if she's going to stay awake. I don't move her, though. She can lean on me for however long she wants.

Neither one of us move as vampires and werewolves battle each other across the screen. All but two. There's an instant attraction between them, and it's odd but also refreshing. Never has a movie grabbed my interest the way this one has. There's romance, of course, but also action and betrayal. I can

see why she likes it so much. The movie ends with the promise
of a sequel.

The credits roll and she scoots over to look at me. "So,
what did you think?"

"It was pretty good."

"That's it? It's one of my all-time favorites."

"Maybe next time we can watch the next one."

Her cheshire grin is everything. "So, you did like it."

"Yes, I liked it." I glance at the clock. It's not late, but I
don't know how tired she is. "I should probably go so you can
get some rest."

"Oh," the smile has vanished. "Yeah, okay."

I'm not sure how to go about this. It's not something
we've talked about, and don't know if I should just get up and
leave. Give her a hug? What's the protocol?

Standing, I hover by the couch, waiting for her to take the
lead. She doesn't move for a second, and I take a step toward
the door. For whatever reason, that seems to spur her into
action. "Can I see you tomorrow?"

"I don't know," she tucks a piece of hair behind her ear.
"I'm not sure what time David will be home."

"Oh, okay." I try not to let disappointment hit me, but it's
hard. I was hoping to take her to breakfast.

She walks me to the door and puts her arms around my
waist. Hug it is. I'm okay with hugging. "Thank you for
dinner tonight. This is probably the most fun staying in I've
had in a long time."

"I'm glad I could provide that for you." My arms go
around her because I feel like an idiot having them hang at my
sides.

She leans her head back and smiles. It's honest and I know
she's not putting on an act to make me feel better. What I
don't expect is for her to lift up on her toes and press her lips
against mine.

It's awkward and it shouldn't be. Yet another instance where I'm not sure how I should handle myself. She pulls back quickly and covers her mouth with her hand. "I'm so sorry. I'm not sure what came over me. I don't usually do things like this." She takes a step back and lowers her eyes to the ground. "I never do anything like this, actually."

She shouldn't be ashamed to be attracted to someone and act on it. I can't allow her to think she did anything wrong. She didn't. I step toward her and lift her chin until I can see her eyes. "There's nothing wrong with a kiss."

"But you didn't react."

"I'm following you when it comes to anything physical. You've said quite a few times that you want this to be appearances only, and I'm trying to respect that." I pause for a moment to make sure she's listening to what I'm saying. "But if you want something physical, I'm more than okay with that. You are beautiful inside and out. All you have to do is tell me what you want."

"You." The word is rushed and she throws her arms around my neck and her lips smash into mine. I put all my weight on my heels to keep from falling backward, but wrap my arms around her waist to pull her closer.

This isn't what I was expecting, but I'm also not going to argue. She deepens the kiss, her tongue exploring mine, and one of her hands goes into my hair, gripping it tightly. I can't help but wonder how long she's kept this passion pent up, waiting for someone to unleash it on.

I pull her even closer until our bodies meld to each other. She moans into my mouth, and it is everything. Knowing something as simple as a kiss and being held are what turns her on is something I'll keep in the back of my mind.

Her mouth doesn't leave mine as she puts some space between us, pulling at the bottom of my shirt. She pulls away long enough to yank it over my head and throw it on the floor, and her lips are back on mine.

Unsure of where her bedroom is, I move us toward the couch. The living room is dark, but the glow of the light over the sink is enough for me to guide us without bumping into anything. Her fingers toy with the button on my jeans, and I place a hand over them, breaking our kiss. "Are you sure?"

"Yes." The word is almost a growl and fuck if it doesn't turn me on. I push off my shoes and she unbuttons my jeans and pushes them down. My underwear and socks are the only things left on my body, and she's fully clothed.

"Your turn," I smirk. She fiddles with the waist of her pants and starts to push them down, but I stop her. "Let me."

She stops but puts her arms around her stomach and her eyes are looking around the room. Anything from having to meet my eyes. "I think I want to leave this on."

There's no need to be self-conscious, but if that's what she wants, I'll abide. "Okay, but just so you know, you deserve to have every inch of you worshiped."

Grabbing the top of her pants, I rub my knuckles against her skin and the shiver in response pushes me forward. I pull them down, along with her panties, bending until I'm on my knees in front of her. She steps out of them and I turn her until she's standing in front of the couch, and motion for her to sit down. Her eyes are on me, no doubt wondering what I'll do next. "I don't have a condom."

"That isn't something we need to worry about right now."

"What do you me—." My lips pressing quick small kisses along her calves, breaks off her question. I have a condom in my wallet, but tonight is about her. Making her feel good.

Spreading her legs, I nestle between them. All of her on display, and it's going to take everything in me to take my time. My hand slides along her other leg, slow and measured.

The roughness between my hand and her soft skin, a friction that makes her squirm.

I continue my trail of kisses, pausing to place one behind her knee before putting her leg over my shoulder. My other hand glides down her leg, coming to a stop over her pussy. And oh my God, she is drenched. How long has it been since someone took care of her without putting all the focus on themself?

Her breath hitches as I rub my thumb over her clit. A quick glance up and her head is leaned back. Her focus on the ceiling. I pause, pulling my lips away from her thigh, but my thumb still circling her. "Eyes on me."

Her head snaps forward and she does as she's asked. Even in the darkness, I can feel her light brown eyes on mine. I nip at her thigh before kissing the pain away and feel her legs tighten around me. The kisses continue until I've worked my way to my target.

I look up one more time to make sure she's watching. To make sure she knows exactly who is about to make her forget anyone before me, and not want anyone after me. She doesn't disappoint, gaze trained on me.

I replace my thumb with my mouth. My tongue circling and sucking. Caroline moves her other leg until it's over my shoulder and slides herself down the couch, pushing herself as close to my mouth as possible.

I slide two fingers inside her, and move my other hand to her face. Her chin in my palm so her eyes meet mine. She grips my hair with one hand and holds my hand with the other while circling my thumb with her tongue. Jesus, I'm going to come before her.

Her hips move in a circular motion, creating friction where she needs it, and I let her take the lead. As much as I want to prolong her pleasure, I know she isn't going to last much longer. She needs a release, and I'll be damned if I'm not going to give it to her.

Pumping my fingers inside her, I increase the pressure of my tongue on her clit. She pulls my hair and throws her head back as she rides out her orgasm.

Before I have a chance to say, or do, anything, she pushes the coffee table away with her feet, and forces me back. "Condom?"

I reach for my jeans and the wallet inside the back pocket. As soon as I have it, she rips it from my hands, pulls down my underwear and slides the latex on my cock. My goal tonight was to make her feel cherished, but she's taken control, and slides over me. My back is against the wood floor and she rides me until I'm panting.

My hands go to her hips to slow her movements. Anything to keep me from coming right this second, but she knocks them away. Leaning over me she kisses my neck, working her way to my lips. Her tongue plunges into my mouth, dancing with mine. I need to come...now. I grab her hips and pull her as close to me as possible, riding me until I see stars. I let go, and move a hand between us, working her clit until she comes once again.

Sex with this woman I'm just getting to know should not be this intense, or perfect, but yet it is. She lays down on top of me and until her breathing is under control. "You make me do things I wouldn't normally do."

"I could say the same for you."

17

caroline

IT'S BEEN two days since I've seen Carlos and I keep replaying Saturday night over and over again. It's been my nightly memory before going to bed, and I don't know what came over me that night, but I don't regret it one bit.

He took care of me in a way that Nathan never did. His focus one hundred percent on what I was feeling. Hell, I don't think he was even going to go past going down on me until I essentially jumped his bones. I giggle to myself before remembering I'm at work. Not only that, I need to remember I can't develop actual feelings for the man. No matter how much we text each other or talk on the phone. Or how he makes me feel like I'm more than just a mom. I'm a woman who can enjoy things outside of parenting.

The bell above the door jingles and Kate walks in. "God, can you quit smiling? It's annoying."

Crap. Smiling all the time isn't a good thing when I'm trying to keep my heart at bay. "Sorry, but y'all are the ones who pushed me to go on a date with Carlos." I shrug my shoulders. "Is the van ready for the flowers?"

"Yep. And we said a date. Not walking around all starry eyed." She comes around the counter and looks over the arrangements that were ordered. "I hate delivering for funerals."

"Me too. I'm glad you drew the short straw this time around." Her other comment is not worth responding to.

"I bet," she grumbles. "Can you grab a few stands while I load these? The only plus side, is the funeral director sets it up. I can drop and run because dead bodies freak me out."

I go to the back of the shop and get the flower stands she requested. The funeral home typically has some, but we like to take a few with us just in case. Instead of stopping at the counter, I walk out the front door and hand them to Kate. "Thanks," she sighs. "Where are Sam and Emily?"

"They went to lunch early so I can meet Carlos during my lunch."

"You're seeing him more than I expected."

I nod. "Mornings and mid-day are all we have to see each other with our work hours."

"Are you going to introduce him to David? Or even the rest of your family?"

"Pfft. Most of my family frequents the bar at some point during the week so they know who he is. As for David, not yet." Not ever if we end things within a reasonable time. Though after the other night, I don't know that I want things to end. At least not the physical part of it.

"I can understand that. You want to protect him in case things don't work out." She opens the van door and slides in. "But as a product of divorced parents, you don't want to wait forever if you see a future with this guy. If David finds out from someone else, it's going to be devastating." She closes the door, starts the engine, and drives away.

That thought never occurred to me. I'm not sure if that makes me an awful mother, but up until him bringing food to my house, I never thought I'd feel anything but friendship for Carlos. Now, I don't know. The lines are already starting to blur and it's barely been a week. Eventually I'll have to ask Carlos what he thinks. Right now, though, I want to feel giddy in a way I haven't felt in way too long.

* * *

"How has your work day been so far?" Carlos sits down next to me at one of the tables. We're meeting at Out of the Ashes. He's working the morning and afternoon shift, and it's just easier.

"It's been okay, I guess." I shrug and take a drink of my sweet tea. "Had to get flowers ready for a funeral, which is never fun."

"I'm sorry."

"Don't be. It's part of the job. Flowers aren't just for happily ever afters."

"True, but they should be." He takes a drink of his water. This is the part that sucks about lunch dates, we both have to go back to work afterward.

"How's your day?" I ask. "Any chance you've talked Patrick into making us steaks? I feel the need to compare."

Carlos chuckles and shakes his head. "He said he's only making what's on the menu, and steaks aren't. Basically, we're screwed."

"Maybe not," I shrug. "I've been known to be pretty good on the grill."

"Really?" I can't tell if his tone is mocking or not.

"Women are perfectly capable of grilling. I'm sure Angie did it a lot here."

"Only for a little bit. She's not the world's best cook, but she does enough to get by if she has to." He clears his throat, "and I wasn't insinuating you couldn't grill. I just haven't met a lot of women who enjoy it."

"I taught myself. With burgers the first time, and the flames went so high, I thought I burned off my eyebrows."

"That sounds like a challenge." Carlos rubs his hands together like an evil villain.

Before I have a chance to respond, Eric shows up with two plates of food. "Buffalo wings all around," he grins. He holds up two small packets, "I even brought you wet wipes because I'm not a jerk."

"Wait, you don't give them to everyone?"

He shrugs and turns back toward the bar. "Depends if I like them or not."

"Is he telling the truth?" I whisper to Carlos. I feel bad for the people if it is.

"No. He rarely gives people their food." He picks up a wing out of his basket and grins. "So back to the challenge."

"I never agreed to a challenge." The last thing I want to do is cook on a date.

"Come on," he smirks. "I'll make it easy for you and let you decide what we're cooking."

"That's not the problem." Well, besides the fact I don't want to cook unless I have to. "Who is going to judge our meal? Neither one of us is going to give honest feedback."

He places his hands over his heart. "You wound me. I'd never take advantage during a cooking challenge."

"Okay," I snort. I pick up a wing and devour it. My friends would be gasping in horror. They are very much the type that eat less in front of their dates. I don't have that luxury. Whoever dates me has to take me as I am because I'm not changing for anyone. I've been down that road before. Besides, he's not my real boyfriend. He's more like a friend, with bene-fits apparently, and I'm more relaxed around him.

"Seriously, you choose what you want to cook. And if you insist on a judge, we can do a double date with Angie and Dylan. It's not like Dylan would side with me without tasting the food. We had a bit of a rocky start when he came back to town. They'll be our judges."

He's got a point. "And when would we do this? David has football games Saturday mornings and you work the night shift. It's not like we have all the time in the world."

"How about a Sunday? That is if you can find a sitter. If not, it'll just go on the board for another time when we can."

I let the idea roll through my head. "Assuming we're still doing this thing when football season is over, you're on." I eat another wing. "And prepare to lose to my mad grilling skills."

"In your dreams."

I like the playful banter. It's something I've never experienced outside of my family and friends. Nathan was always so serious and would shut it down. Looking back, with how close my family was, I don't know how I ever ended up with him.

My phone dings and I glance at the screen. It's Kate, back from the funeral home.

Kate: When are you going to be back in?

I should answer it, but I don't.

"Do you need to get that?" Carlos points toward my phone. It vibrated again as a reminder. I should really turn that feature off.

"Nope." I shake my head, "the three of them will be fine without me for a little longer."

"Okay." He glances at the TV above the bar. They aren't usually on at night, but during the day it replays old sports games. "So, what position does David play in football?"

It's a shock hearing him ask about David. Well, when it's more than needing to find a babysitter. Nathan hasn't asked once about football season, and he's his father. Then again, Carlos is nothing like my shitty ex-husband. "I don't know yet. This is his first year playing. My brother is trying to teach how to be quarterback."

"Ah, so the leader of the team."

"We'll see. This is the first time he's shown any interest in sports and I'm a little out of my element. So, I'll let him try whatever he wants until something sticks."

"That's a good idea," he nods his agreement. "He may not like any of them, but at least you're giving him options."

"I can't take credit for that." My phone dings again, and I ignore it again. "My mom did the same thing for me and my brothers. Reaf excels at art, always has, and Bryce went the football route."

"What about you? What did you do in your youth?"

"None of that. I took the easy way out and stayed in my room to read."

"Makes sense." He picks up his water. "Oh, how much do I owe you for that damaged book? I know the library isn't going to take that back."

"Don't worry about it. I was planning on keeping it anyway and paying for the lost book fee."

"Such a rebel."

"I have my moments." I grin and pick up my phone when it dings for the third time. "Hold on, let me see what they need."

Kate: Seriously, I need to know.

Kate: Nathan is here asking to speak to you.

Oh shit. That's not good. He has barely called in the past three months about his son, and he chooses now to do it. In person of all things.

"I, uh, need to go."

"Is everything okay?"

No, not even a little bit, but he doesn't need to be dragged into whatever is going on. "Yeah. I'll call you later." I lean over the table and give him a quick peck on the cheek.

He does have a point about me running out. This time, it's for good reason. Whatever Nathan wants, it can't be anything good. Especially with this timing.

* * *

It's a good thing the shop isn't too far from the bar. I didn't bother telling Kate I was on my way. That gives him time to prepare whatever the hell he wants with me. No, I need the element of surprise.

Kate is behind the counter with her arms crossed, not at all pleased to be talking to him. He's leaning on the counter with his back to the front door. The only warning he has is the bell above the door as I charge through it. "What are you doing here?"

"Woah," he holds his hands up in surrender. "You're fired up for no reason."

"You're here harassing my friends about where I am, of course I'm angry. You don't call about David in months and miss your days with him, and now you all of a sudden want to talk. What are you playing at?"

Kate waves at me from behind Nathan, silently asking me if I want her to stay for support. I shake my head and she leaves the counter area, but she doesn't leave completely. I see her shadow against the door at the end of the hallway. Even though she isn't listening, I appreciate the gesture just the same.

"I'm not playing at anything. I merely came by to ask for David's football schedule."

"How did you even know about that?"

"I may have heard your brother talking about it when I got my oil changed." Ugh, of course. Reaf was probably telling his coworkers all about it. I can't blame him, though. He couldn't have known this asshole was listening in.

"And that required a visit? I could have easily text you the schedule."

He shrugs, "maybe I wanted to see you."

"I highly doubt that."

"How serious are you and the bartender?" That wasn't a question I was expecting.

"That's not any of your business, Nathan." Of all the things for him to question me on, it's this? "You walked out on me and David a long time ago. You have no right to ask about my personal life. The only reason you have any access to my son at all is because it's required by the law."

"I think I have the right to know who is going to be around our son." He straightens the sleeves of his dress shirt. "And I don't know that having that man around is a good idea."

"Let's face it, you only care because I'm not miserable." I'm not going to tell him that Carlos and David haven't met. It's none of his business. "You need to leave. I'll text you David's schedule for his games and practices. It'd be nice if you showed up to something for our son every once in a while."

He smirks and walks toward the door. I move out of the way, putting as much distance as I can between us in the small store front, "I expect the schedule today."

He walks out with not a care in the world. I don't think I've ever hated someone as much as I do him right now. I wasn't this angry when he left all those years ago. But now that I'm showing one ounce of having a life outside of being a mom, he wants to show up and throw a wrench in everything.

As soon as he's gone Kate comes out of the hallway and stands beside me. "Are you okay?"

I collapse into her, letting her wrap me in a hug. It's not

the same as the ones Carlos gives, but I'll take it. "Nope. Nothing good can come of this."

She leans back, giving me a look over to see if I'm about to fall apart. "Take the rest of the day off. The three of us can handle whatever walk-ins come by."

"I'm fine." Tears flow down my face. Not because of what he said, but because of how angry I am. How he finds a way to make me feel small and like a failure by simply using his words.

"No, you're not. Go home, or go see your mom. Either way I'm texting her to let her know what happened."

"Fine." There's no point in arguing. "And don't worry about texting my mom. I'll go talk to her. Maybe she'll help me find some way out of this mess."

18

carlos

IT TAKES everything in me not to run after her. To make sure everything is okay. Her face turned ash white when she read the message. The kiss on the cheek is the only reason I know it's not something I said.

"I think I'm going to name her runaway girlfriend." Eric comes to the table and helps me pick up what's left of my lunch with Caroline. "Every time I look up, all I see is her back rushing out the door."

"Not now, Eric." I grunt. "I think something happened."

"And you didn't charge after her?"

Thanks for making me feel like shit. "She didn't give me a chance, and I'm not sure if it's my place with all of this being so new."

"That sounds like an excuse, man," he shakes his head and carries the cups to the kitchen. "You need to go after her."

"It's not like I know where she took off to. For all I know, it was something with her son and she's rushing off to pick him up from school. I haven't met the kid yet, and it's really not my place if that's the case."

"You have a point there." He sets the dishes in the sink, and I do the same. "Be sure to call her when you get off. At least to make sure all is well. And, if her son is sick, run by the store and get some things to make him feel better. That will definitely get you some brownie points."

That's the difference between me and him. I'm no longer interested in scoring points to win her over. I'm genuinely concerned about what happened. I think that's something that comes with age. Playing those types of games no longer interest me. "I'll call her later."

Patrick grabs my attention. "She barely touched her food; do you want me to box it up?"

"Sure." I doubt I'll be seeing her to take them to her, but it'll be a nice midnight snack for later.

I pull my phone out of my pocket to see if she's text me. Anything to let me know she's good. Instead, I send her one.

Carlos: Is everything okay? Let me know if you need anything.

She's not likely to respond right away, and I shove my phone back in my pocket. Today is going to be a long day. Not because of the work. No, that goes by quickly, even when you're dealing with repeat customers. The busyness makes time fly. But, because I'll be looking at my phone at every opportunity, waiting for Caroline to respond. I only need to know that she's okay. Every worst-case scenario flashes through my head and it's torture.

* * *

The microwave dings and I pull out the wings. I've been home for two hours and still haven't gotten the courage to call Caroline. Afraid that whatever she had to deal with today will ruin whatever it is we have together.

It hasn't been long, but I feel like we're making progress into more than fake. Into more than being together to keep people off our backs and her ex-husband from making her feel like shit. I've had girlfriends in the past, and sure there was attraction. But the more I'm around Caroline, the more I want to learn about her. The more I want to spend my time with her, and be a part of her life. And bring her into my life. It's terrifying.

My mom and dad have always been my goal when it comes to relationships. Even though Mom doesn't show it, I know him being gone hurts her deeply. They were the couple all my tias would swoon over at gatherings. Every photo, every shaky video from my childhood, has the two of them smiling, or dancing. They truly enjoyed each other's company and I want that for myself.

And I think I've found it, under an illusion for others, and maybe even Caroline herself, but I want that with her. The fact she hasn't called or replied to my text has those dreams dying one by one.

Fuck it. I set the plate of wings on the counter and grab my phone. There's no need for me to wonder if she's okay. I've been fine letting her take the lead, but I need to know she doesn't need me right now.

I find her name on my phone and press call. It rings three times before she answers. "Hello?"

Her voice is scratchy and she sniffles. All is definitely not okay with her. "Hey, are you okay? What happened this afternoon?"

Another sniffle and a sigh. She's about to push me out, I can feel it. "A bunch of stuff with Nathan. He showed up at my job, and then actually came to David's practice tonight.

I'm sorry, I just can't talk right now. I'll call you in the morning."

"Okay." The word isn't all the way out of my mouth before the line goes dead.

I knew him showing up at the bar the other day wasn't a good thing. I've seen his type before. It's something you see often working in bars. He'll do everything he can to make her feel like shit and unworthy of any sort of happiness. It's not something I can stand around and continue to let happen.

Instead of rushing to her house because I'm sure David is still awake. It's still early evening. I call my mom. She'll have answers on how to move forward. In my eyes, she's the gospel on romance and even though I know she'll have a million questions, I've never been in this position before and I'm at a loss.

I press her name, hit call, and put it on speaker. This could take a while and I don't want to hold my phone. "Carlos?" She answers after the first ring. Damn, did she have it sitting beside her? Or, have some sort of sense that I was going to need her today?

"Hey, Mom." I lean against the counter and pick up one of the wings. "I need some help."

"Oh, you do? I thought you didn't need help with anything, and you live to make life easier on your mama."

She acts like I've never asked for her help with anything. I think for a second, and maybe she's right. Not since I was younger. Not even when Dad passed away. I dealt with that by piling on more hours at work, and pretending it didn't happen. Knowing full well it isn't healthy.

"Okay, I'm sorry I've never asked for your help before but it's about a girl."

"The one you've been seeing and refuse to bring for dinner." I'll have to remedy that soon. Especially if we can make it past whatever is going on with Caroline now.

"Yes, Mom."

"What do you need? Is it love making or how to romance her?" I choke on the wing I just took a bite of. Those are words I never want to hear out of her mouth.

"Mom. No. Just no." I cough and take a drink of water to help the food go down. "Something happened today and it has to do with her ex-husband."

"Oh," she gasps. "Are you involved in something messy?"

"No," I sigh and run my fingers through my hair. Maybe calling her was a mistake. "They've been over for years, but after seeing us together he seems to be making life hard for her."

"I see." She pauses for a second. "Mijito, is this girl worth the trouble? I want you to be sure."

"Yes." She's always trying to protect me, even though I'm grown and capable of taking care of myself. I have a feeling that's something a parent never stops doing.

"So, what happened?"

"Honestly, she didn't go into detail just that he showed up at her work and son's practice. He most likely said something and now she's upset, but won't open up."

Mom doesn't say anything for a few moments. I never mentioned her having a kid in any other conversations. "The niño is going to make things harder. She will move heaven and earth to make sure he's protected."

"I know, and she does. But I need to know that she's okay and we are fine. How do I do that without being creepy?"

"Have you met the little boy?"

"Not yet. We hadn't talked about that."

She sighs, and I can imagine her shaking her head. Yes, I know it's an important conversation, but I didn't know if we'd still even be a couple this week, fake or not. "Do you know when he goes to bed?"

"Yes."

Another voice enters the conversation. "You should wait until he's in bed then show up at her house with her favorite treat."

"Mom, do you have me on speaker? Marisol does not need to hear my problems."

"Yes, we do," my other sister, Gabriella adds in. Just great. The both of them will give me grief over this for years.

"It's not a bad idea," my mom concedes. She's clearly siding with them. What is up with the women in my life ganging up on me?

I'll humor them, though. "Do I let her know I'm coming?"

"No." Both of my sister's yell.

"It'll make it more romantic if you don't," Marisol stage whispers. "Take her some ice cream and flowers."

"It's getting cooler at night, why would I take ice cream?"

"Because it's good," Gabby argues.

"Fine. What kind?"

"How are we supposed to know that?" Gabby asks. "She's your girlfriend. But you can never go wrong with cookies and cream."

"Why am I taking advice from my teenage sisters?" I say it low, but not low enough.

"I'm not sure if I should be offended." Marisol gasps. "And because we know romance. You need help, and we want to meet them."

Do I go through with this insane plan? I mean it's better than anything I've got. The worst she can do is tell me to leave and I'll have ice cream that melts on the way home. "Fine. I'll head over there in a couple of hours."

"Don't forget the flowers," Gabby says.

"And let us know what happens." Marisol adds.

My mom is quiet for a moment, probably waiting for my sisters to leave the room. "Good luck, mijito. I hope it works out. And I can't wait to meet the woman who has stolen your heart."

"Goodnight, Mom."

It looks like I have a few stops to make.

* * *

I dress down to go to her house, sweats and a t-shirt. I don't want her to think I've planned this, even though I have. More like agonized over it the past few hours. She doesn't need to know that.

Pulling open a drawer, silverware clacks against each other until I have two spoons in hand. I guess I could buy plastic ones, but I would have to get a whole box and they'd sit there unused for a very long time. I grab my keys off the counter and walk out the door, locking it behind me.

There's a gas station on the way to her house and it's my first stop. The flowers look sad as they sit in the empty store, and I'm not taking her subpar plants. Besides, she probably gets tired of looking at them. I know I would if I worked in a flower shop. Though the same doesn't apply to beer, or liquor. I keep those in stock at home.

There's a small freezer next to the counter, and I look through the options. Most of them are ice creams on a stick, and I don't want those to melt on the way over. Not that the other won't, but at least it's contained.

I finally spot the ice cream my sister suggested and grab two of them. If she's anything like Marisol, she won't be keen on sharing with me. I debate getting another six pack of beer, but the sound of that and ice cream isn't appealing.

I set the pints on the counter and almost have a heart attack when the cashier gives me the price. I could have gotten a bigger size at the grocery store for what I'm paying here. It's worth it, though. If this small gesture manages to put a smile on Caroline's face, I'll consider it a win.

The sky is pitch black as I drive to the outskirts of Asheville. Her house is in the country, and I never realized how creepy it is when you're the only person on the road.

Her driveway is coming up, and I turn off my high beams so I don't blind her when I pull up. With the car in park, I debate how to go about this. Do I knock on the door? Call her?

In the end I settle on a simple text. This will either be an epic fail; or it won't. There's only one way to find out.

Carlos: Come outside.

19

caroline

I WILL NEVER UNDERSTAND why Nathan can't just go on living his life without a thought of what I'm doing. He hasn't been around for literal months and now...because he sees me with someone, he feels the need to be involved in David's life. He's using our child to get to me. To make me feel like shit, and I don't know what to do.

But this right here is exactly what he wants. Me sitting on my couch once David is in bed, crying into my glass of wine, questioning if dating someone makes me a bad mother.

The double standard is such bullshit. He has been with so many women since we split up. Taken David around them when he actually decides he wants to show him off as if he's some sort of trophy. That being there for him, when it suits his own agenda, makes him an amazing father.

I'm so tired of all of it. Having to be strong for my son when all I want to do is sit in my closet to catch my breath. Having to come up with lies as to why his dad can't make it to this thing or that. Or even simply show up to pick him up when he's supposed to have him.

But the last straw was Nathan asking him what he thought about my new boyfriend after football practice. Seeing the confusion cross my son's face and looking at me as if I'm the liar. That was too much to bear. That was the breaking point, and why I'm a bottle into my wine stash. Why I'll have a hell of a hangover tomorrow and suffer through it because I deserve it.

My phone vibrates on the table, and I debate whether or not to answer it. I'm sure it's my friends, or mom, calling to check in on me. But the sound of a car in my driveway has me second guessing. It could be Nathan here to pour more alcohol into the wound. If that's the case, I'll call the cops and have them make him leave. He has no right being here on when it's not his day to pick up David.

It's not, though. It's from Carlos.

Carlos: Come outside.

No, he can't be here. Not only because of David. I'm an absolute mess. I swipe until the camera on my phone comes up and check my reflection. Mascara is dried under my puffy eyes and the bun I put my hair in earlier has fallen to the side. It reminds me of those first few months after David was born and this was the best I could do.

Caroline: Be there in a min

I don't know why I responded. Hell, I don't know if I'm ready to have this conversation. But he came all this way, and I feel like I owe him something after running out on him yet again.

Rushing to the bathroom, I grab a hand towel, put it

under the faucet to wet it, and scrub under my eyes. This is probably going to look worse, but I don't care. I need to get the mascara off my face. As broken down as I feel right now, I don't want Carlos knowing how Nathan's actions affect me.

A quick glance in the mirror, and it's good enough. Besides, it's dark and he won't be able to see my face all that well. I turn off the light and head toward the front door. Shit, I need my wine. I'm not sure what the rest of the night will consist of, but emergency wine is always a good call. I run to the kitchen and grab a bottle, the corkscrew and go back to the front door.

Inhale, exhale. There's no need to be nervous. Opening the door, I walk onto the porch, except his car isn't running anymore. "That was more than a minute."

It takes everything in me not to shriek because I don't want to wake David, but the corkscrew flies out of my hand. At least it's not the wine. "Why are you sitting in the dark like a creeper?"

"Sorry, I didn't really want to sit in the car anymore, and figured I'd sit on one of the porch chairs." I can see the shadow of his head look around. "You should really put a light out here."

Sighing, I set the bottle of wine on the table, and search the porch for the corkscrew. Bringing this out here would be useless without it. "I have one, but bugs fly around it and I don't like being hit in the face with them when I come out."

"That's valid." He agrees and bends down. "Looking for this?"

"Yep." I grab it out of his hand and sit in the chair next to him. Pulling the wine bottle into my lap, I open it with the corkscrew and set those on the table. Without missing a beat, I drink straight from the bottle.

"That kind of day, huh?" He hands me something and it's cold when I wrap my hand around it.

"You have no idea." I pull the container closer to my face and a small smile slip through when I realize it's ice cream. With all the chaos in my life, and my lack of opening up, he continues going out of his way to make things easier for me.

He grabs the bottle of wine from my hand, sets it on the table, and gives me a spoon. "You know you can talk to me, right? No matter what you have going on, you aren't going to scare me away from anything. Even if it includes your pendejo ex."

I giggle because even though I don't speak Spanish, I know what that word means, and it's appropriate on so many levels. "Are you sure? Because this might."

"I have two teenage sisters, and nothing that has come out of their mouths has frightened me, though it probably should."

"That only means you are a good big brother."

"What happened?"

I fill him in on Nathan coming to the shop and acting like an entitled ass. Taking ice cream and wine breaks to give me breaks. Then I hit him with the whammy.

"He came over to me and David after practice. I assumed it was to tell him bye, but no. He asked David what he thought about you." I look over at Carlos and his mouth is wide open, just as shocked as I was when I heard it. "If you could have seen the look on David's face. It was like he felt betrayed because I share so many things with him, but I hadn't shared you, yet. But the only reason I didn't is because I didn't know what this is. Not any official sense."

Carlos is looking at the ground. No doubt gathering his thoughts. The crickets chirping beneath the halfmoon our symphony. The melancholy feel of it definitely fits my mood.

I don't know whether I'm winning or losing when it comes to life lately. Things were simpler when David was the sole focus of my attention, but as much as I try to fight feeling an emotion toward Carlos, I can't help it. There's a void in my life, and he's filling the gap perfectly.

"Do you want me to meet David?"

Do I? I mean obviously I need to introduce them after tonight. "When we first came up with this whole thing...no, I didn't. What was the point in him meeting someone that wouldn't be sticking around?"

"What about now?" Even though I can only see his outline, I know his full focus is on me.

"Now...yes, I think so. Not only because of what happened tonight. But I don't think the word fake really applies to us anymore. Not after what happened in my living room the other night, and definitely not with how I'm starting to feel about you."

"And how is that?" He sets his ice cream on the table, and I no longer hear the crickets. It's as if the universe is holding its breath, waiting for my answer.

"I can't stop thinking about you. My mom used to be the first person I talked to every day, other than David, and now, it's you. And it's not just about the sex, even though that was mind-blowing and I hope we do that again soon. You actually care about me."

I set my ice cream next to his on the table and grab the wine bottle, taking another swig for liquid courage. "Like tonight. I pretty much hung up on you earlier because I couldn't handle myself, and you showed up with ice cream and a listening ear. Who does that?"

"Normal guys who aren't assholes?"

I go on as if I didn't hear him. "And the other night, I didn't feel like going out for our date, and you made the perfect spread, cleaned up the mess I made, and made everything feel perfect. You're not some machine program inside a body made to fulfill a woman's dream, are you?"

He chuckles, "I'll have to double check with my mom, but no, I don't think so."

"Are you sure? Because there is no way a person is this caring or amazing after a few first dates. Especially with all the drama that keeps coming up in my life."

I'm not sure when he stood up, but he's standing in front of me. He places his hands on either said of my face to keep my attention on him. "Caroline, stop."

He presses his lips to mine and I melt into him. His tongue slides across the seam of my lips, asking for entrance and I allow it. This is nothing like the frantic kisses we shared over the weekend. The exploration is slow, sensual, and he's taking his time. If this is how he plans on stopping my tirades in the future, I'm completely okay with it.

I reach around him to set the bottle on the table, almost missing it, before wrapping my arms around him. He backs up until he hits the chair and sits down, pulling me on top of him. My knees slide on either side of him, and he moves his hands to my ass to keep me from sliding backward.

The wine is working its way through my body, and I might be slightly drunk, but that doesn't mean I don't know what I'm doing. The other night he showed me I can take what I want, and it was freeing. My hips move over him, and his grip tightens.

He breaks the kiss, pulling back the tiniest fraction. "Maybe this isn't the best idea." He's panting and I know he wants this as much as I do. "We both have work tomorrow and David is inside sleeping."

Damn it. He has a point. Why does he have to be the voice of reason? I press one last kiss to his lips and climb off him. From the bulge in his sweats, I wasn't the only one turned on. "Fine, but we'll need to continue this at some other point."

"Agreed." He stands and puts distance between us. "Also, I have an idea of how I can meet David in a lower pressure way."

Talk about switching the subject. "And what is that?"

"Well, obviously it doesn't need to be in a space where Nathan can show up. But, my mom does family dinners on Sunday nights. Y'all can come over for that and my sisters can play with David."

"Aren't they teenagers?"

"Yeah, but they want to meet both of you. And they are good with kids. They volunteer at any camps for smaller kids in their school district."

"I don't know." The thought of meeting his family is terrifying, but he's right. It's low stress and David won't be bored.

"If you feel uncomfortable you can leave. We can drive over together and I'll meet him before the family, or you can come on your own and I'll meet him there. It's up to you."

"Okay. I'll let you know when it gets closer." I glance at my watch and realize it's past midnight. "I should probably go to bed."

"Me too." He takes a step forward and presses a kiss to my cheek. But his arms are keeping a distance between us. "I'll call or text in the morning. Goodnight, Care."

"Night, Carlos." I watch him as he gets in his car and pulls away. My half empty wine bottle and the two pints of ice cream are still on the table. The ice cream melted and I pick everything up before heading inside.

Well, I guess after tonight we're a real couple. I may regret it one day, but I deserve happiness as much as the next person. And I think Carlos could be that. Only time will tell.

20

carlos

"IS SHE HERE YET?" I yell from the kitchen. Mom and I are making the last of the tortillas. I could have gotten away without helping, but this was my idea and it's only fair.

"No," Marisol snaps back. "If you ask again, I'm going to muzzle you."

"Why is she so violent?" I ask Mom as she rolls out another ball of dough.

"I blame it on the video games she plays."

"Maybe don't let her play those in the future." I flip one of the tortillas in the rotation. We have 3 comals going and the last burner has carne asada simmering. The house smells delicious. It's a weekly thing, but I remember growing up it smelling like it every day. Aside from seeing my family every day, and not being around much when my sisters were little, this is one of the things I miss most about being on my own.

"Oh, now you're going to parent me?" She puts a flat piece of dough in one of the pans I just emptied. "Just you wait. If things work out with this girl, you'll understand how hard it is to raise little ones."

"He's not that little. I think he's around seven."

"Fine, you get some of the fun years, but don't let those fool you. Teenagers are fun and scary at the same time."

"I heard that," Marisol hollers.

"You were supposed to." Mom finishes rolling the last of the tortillas. The only thing left is the rice.

"Hey, there's a car coming down the road I don't recognize." Gabriela yells to nobody in particular.

I run from the kitchen to the living room and push Marisol out of the way to look out the window. "Where?"

"Dude, what the hell?" Marisol shoves me.

"Mari, stop cussing. You know I don't like it." Mom's voice is stern, and I have a feeling this is a battle she has with her constantly.

"Yeah, stop cussing." I peer out the window, and it's her. Caroline is driving slowly up the road, looking at the mailbox numbers. A part of me wants to run out to the front yard to let her know this is the right house, but I feel like that would seem a bit desperate.

Both of my sisters fall into a fit of giggles. "You've got it bad. I thought our friend's got googly eyed, but you are something else." Gabi says through laughter.

"Shut up."

"Yeah, that's not going to happen big bro. You're the one acting like a teenage girl." I swear I'm going to murder both of them before the night is over.

Rather than sit here and argue with them, I go back to the kitchen to see if Mom needs any more help. But she motions me away. "I'm almost done. Go to the living room unless you want your sisters answering the door when she knocks."

"Good point." I go back to living room to intercept the door, but I'm too late. I didn't even hear Caroline knock. Her hand is raised mid-air and her eyebrows are scrunched together. "Hey, Caroline. These are my sisters, Marisol and Gabriela."

Both girls beam up at her, and take a step back. I'm not sure what protocol is here. Do I hug her or wait to see what she does? She walks inside with a little boy attached to her side. When he sees me, he eyes me wearily. Yeah, it's probably a good idea I didn't go in for a hug right away. "It's nice to meet both of you," she tells my sisters. "This is my son, David."

Both of them bend down to tell him hi, and I swear it's like a flip switched in those two. They aren't the annoying teenagers they were two minutes ago.

Caroline and David come further into the room and stop in front of me. "Hi, David, I'm Carlos."

"I know." Even though his voice is soft, it's sure and there's no room for argument. "You're my mom's boyfriend."

"Yes, I am. It's nice to meet you." I hold out my hand. He has to know that even though he's young, I still intend to treat him with the utmost respect.

He places his hand in mine, shaking it as firmly as he can. "You too."

"Would you like to meet my mom?"

He looks up to Caroline, and when she nods, he says, "Yes."

David seems very well-mannered, at least compared to any kids I know. I wonder if Caroline talked to him on the way over, or if he's nervous. It's most likely a mixture of the two. I can't imagine what he must be feeling meeting people he's never known before.

I lead both of them in the kitchen and my sisters follow behind, curious how the interaction is going to go. "David, Caroline, this is my mom, Raquel."

"Hi, Ms. Raquel," David holds out his hand to shake, but my mom pulls him into a hug. She doesn't do handshakes and never has. David's body is tense for a second but relaxes in her hold. She has that effect on people.

She lets David go, then wraps her arms around Caroline. "It's nice to meet you. I've heard so much about you."

Caroline shoots me a panicked look over my mom's shoulder. "It's nice to meet you."

"Don't worry." I laugh, "I didn't tell her anything bad."

She glares at me before stepping back when Mom releases her. "I'm sure you didn't."

"I hope you're hungry. The food will be ready soon." She nods toward the back door. "I bought a football and some things the kids can play with outside, if you don't want to hang out in here."

"You didn't have to do that?"

"I hope we get to see more of you, and we need to have things for David to do."

Caroline's eyes are watery and I know that small action means the world to her. "Thank you." She gives my mom another hug before leading David out the door.

"I like her." Mom walks back to the stove and stirs the rice. "Don't screw it up."

"You barely know her mom." I roll my eyes and head to the back door.

"She has positive energy." She shoos me out of the kitchen so she can get back to cooking. "I'll call you when it's ready."

Well, my mom won David over...now it's time to see if he'll accept me. This whole evening could go one of two ways and I really need it to go well.

* * *

Caroline is sitting in a chair off the side with my mom. Both of them are chatting and watching us play cornhole. I'm not a huge fan of this game. Never have been because I suck at it.

My tios don't let me live that fact down either. They always put me on the team of whomever they aren't on great terms with at the time.

Hell, even tonight my sisters were fighting over who was going to have to take me. But it's fine. They knew one of them had to because I needed to be on the same side as David. But now we're part way through a game, and I don't know how to talk to him. Maybe I should hang out with more people who have kids.

He breaks the awkward silence between us first. "So, you like my mom?"

This kid is definitely more of a man than I am. He goes in for the kill. "Yes, I do, very much."

I can feel his eyes on me as I throw the bag across the yard, missing the target completely. "Will you be mean to her?"

That catches me completely off guard, and I'm not sure what to do with the question. He could be trying to mess with my mind to ensure he wins, but if he's been watching, that's going to happen anyway. He has to know I'm horrible. The other implication is he knows how his actual father treats his mom, and he doesn't like it. I know Caroline tries to keep her cool in front of David, I've never seen it, but that's the type of mother I'm sure she is. Kids, though...they're perceptive. "I don't plan on it."

He studies me before throwing his bag, his gaze moving from head to toe then back on my face again. Squinting his eyes, he makes whatever judgement he's going to about me. "Okay."

It's not a glowing endorsement, but I'll take it. I know dating her comes with David, and I'm okay with that. There's no doubt in my mind I'll fuck up around him sometimes. I can only hope they both will give me some grace. "Okay."

"Prepare to lose worse than you are now." He tosses the bag and it goes straight into the hole. This kid is either lucky, or he's going to make one hell of a quarter back. Without a doubt, it's the latter.

"See, what I meant," Marisol yells across the yard once she sees the small progress, I've made with him. I toss the bag and hit the side of the board. "He sucks, and you stuck him with me. It's not fair."

Gabi rolls her eyes. "Get over it. I got stuck with him last time. It's exactly fair. We should keep rotating whose team he's on every time we play."

Mom sensed the battle is about to begin, "Girls, that's enough. The game needs to end soon anyway. I'm sure everyone here has school tomorrow."

All three of them groan. David looks over at me, "Game point?"

"Sure." We could go five more rounds, and it wouldn't change the fact they are going to win, and we're going to lose.

"Go ahead, David." Marisol sighs. "Even if you missed, there's no way in hell we'd win."

"Language, Mari." My mother's voice is stern. "After David's throw, I think we need to call it a night." She shoots a glare at my sister for her behavior.

Marisol doesn't say anything else. Simply nods and waits for David to throw the bag. He takes a deep breath and throws the bag. It lands in the hole again. "I'm going to need lessons from you."

"Next time," David nods before turning toward his mom. "I'm going to help clean this up."

The shock that crosses over her face is comical. I have a feeling he doesn't offer to clean often. "Okay."

He runs off to gather the boards while my sisters pick up the bags. They head to the small storage shed I built for my mom a few months ago. Mom excuses herself to go inside, leaving us alone for a few moments. "How did I do?"

She leans forward in her chair as I sit on the ground beside her. "I think you did well. He definitely seems to like your sisters."

"I don't know why. They are a pain in the ass."

She smacks my arm. "Be nice. It'll get better once they are older. My brothers and I fought like cats and dogs, but now we talk more than we ever did."

"That day can't come soon enough." I stand and help her out of the chair. "Maybe the three of us can do something without my sisters, though."

"I think that sounds like a good plan, especially so he can get to know you one on one." The shed door closes, and David comes running over to us. "Let's tell everyone bye so we can get you into bed."

"Okay." He hangs his head. I'll take that as a sign he doesn't want to leave. He walks ahead of us inside and goes to my mom giving her a big hug. "Bye. Thank you for dinner."

"You're very welcome, Mijito."

He leans back and looks up at her. "What does that mean?"

"It's an endearment. It means my little boy."

The grin that takes over David's face is the widest I've seen all night. "I like that." He heads toward the living room to tell my sisters goodbye.

"Thank you so much for dinner. It was amazing." Caroline wraps her in a hug.

"It was nothing." Mom gives her a tight squeeze. "Let me know when you'll be back."

"I will." Caroline grabs my hand and we head toward the living room. "It was nice meeting you."

My sisters don't wave. They surround us in a group hug. "You have to come back."

"We will." She manages to wiggle out. "We better get on the road."

David opens the door and waits for us to walk out before

closing it. The sounds of the suburbs surround us. Cars driving down the road to get home, and kids on bikes hurrying home before their parents call for them.

"Thank you for setting this up," Caroline says as David climbs into the backseat of her car.

"Anytime. Maybe next time we can go out for dinner or something."

"It's a deal." She leans up and wraps her arms around my neck. I want to kiss her so badly, but I'm not sure how much affection she wants to show in front of her son. She gives me a peck on the cheek before letting go. "I'll call you when I get home."

She slides into the car and turns on the engine. "Be careful," I yell before she has the door all the way shut.

"I will." I watch her back into the road, then keep my eyes on the taillights as she drives down the street.

When I turn around, both of my sisters are staring out the window. I'm never going to hear the end of their torment. It's worth it, though. Now to plan an outing for the three of us.

21

caroline

ALL DAVID HAS TALKED about this week is going back to Ms. Raquel's house to Carlos's sisters. He's definitely taken a liking to them and I don't blame him. They remind me a lot of my brothers.

"Mom," David yells, "I can't find my cleats."

"Did you look in your closet?" I swear this child loses everything, and we're already running late for practice.

He rushes down the hall with his cleats in his hand. "I found them. Can we go now?"

"Yep, let me grab my bag and book." I scoop my book off the table and the bag off the couch, stuffing the book inside as I head toward the door. "You got everything?"

"Yes, Mom." He waves the cleats in one hand and his water jug in the other. "Is Dad coming to my practice? He told me he was going to try."

"I'm not sure." The only plus side is he said he'd try and didn't tell him he'd be there for sure. It'd be another disappointment for our son. "He hasn't said anything to me, but I bet he'll try as hard as he can."

"Okay. What about Carlos? Will he be there?" There's no venom or bite. I think he genuinely likes Carlos. I don't know what they talked about last weekend at Raquel's, but whatever it was, it must have put David's worry at ease.

"As long as he's not working."

"I hope he isn't. He said I was going to be an amazing quarterback after watching me play cornhole."

"Looks like Uncle Bryce's coaching is paying off."

He nods vigorously as I shut the door behind us and lock it. "I hope he can make it to a game. If college isn't too busy for him."

"He will. He's bugging me for a schedule. Between all of us, you'll have an entire cheering section just for you."

He gets in the car and babbles on about football plays and his friends on the way to the field. I have no idea what any of it means, even though Bryce played the entire time he was in school. I'll listen, though. These moments don't last forever and I'll take whatever he'll give me.

As soon as we pull up, he jumps out of the car as soon as I have it in park. I sit in the car for a few moments to see if Nathan did show up. I don't see him, and turn the car off. There's a chair I keep in the trunk, and I grab it before sitting on the side of the field.

Realistically I should probably socialize with some of the other parents, but I'd much rather read my book than talk. I have to socialize all day at the flower shop, and this is the small bit of downtime I have to myself. I do need to get with them for snack rotation and all that, but I'll do that toward the end of practice. My book boyfriend is calling my name.

The coach's whistle becomes background noise as I lose myself to the pages. Nothing exists around me except the words I'm taking in. I'm so engrossed in my book that I don't notice the shadow fall over me.

"Hey, whatcha reading?"

I drop my book at the sound of his voice and lose my page. "You've really got to stop making me mess up my books." I smile up at Carlos. "You better hope I can find my page."

"Oh, I have no doubt you will." He leans down and places a kiss on my forehead before taking a seat on the ground beside me.

"Are you already off work? I thought you worked late tonight."

"I have to go back, but I'm using this time as my lunch break."

"You didn't have to do that." I pick up my book, thumbing through the pages until I find the general area, I was in.

"I know, but I told David I'd try to make it to his practice." He looks up at me, shielding his eyes from the sun with his hand. "Why aren't you sitting on the bleachers with all the other parents?"

Sighing, I slide my book back into my bag. "I didn't want to socialize. But that looks kind of bitchy, doesn't it?"

"I'm no expert, but maybe a little?" He turns his gaze toward the field, looking for David. "But that's your prerogative. If you don't want to, then don't."

"I'll have to get better about that. It's not like I don't know any of them. Most of us went to school together, but when Nathan and I split, they definitely picked sides."

"People are dumb when they are young."

"That's for sure," I mutter.

"I definitely think he has a shot at being quarterback," he nods to where David is throwing the football.

"So does my brother." A figure approaching the bleachers

catches my eye, and my body goes rigid. "Well, looks like he decided to show up after all."

Carlos leans forward to see who I'm talking about and groans. "He's not going to start anything will he?"

"In public? Never. He'll probably text me his rant later on." I lean back and try to relax my body. "It's what he usually does when he sees something that he doesn't like."

"I can always go back to work. I don't want to make things difficult for you."

"No." My voice is louder than I anticipated and captures the attention of a few parents. Nathan is also glaring in my direction. "No," I lower my voice. "I don't want you to go. You are one of the few people I find solace with. You also make me ridiculously happy. To hell with what other people think."

"Even Nathan?" His voice shakes, and I know it's out of his own curiosity. The need for reassurance.

"Even him."

He places his hand on my knee and gives it a small squeeze. Both of us watch David's practice until the last whistle blows and he comes running off the field. "You came!"

"I sure did. That quarterback spot is yours."

"I hope so. Uncle Bryce will be so happy if it is."

Carlos holds his hand out to David to give him a shake. "I have to get back to work, but maybe the three of us can go out for ice cream this weekend."

David bypasses his hand and gives him a hug. "Thank you for coming."

"Anytime. As soon as we have your game schedule, I'll see what I can do to be there." He gives me a quick peck on the cheek. "I'll call you later." And he walks away.

"So, things are getting serious with the two of you?" Ugh, Nathan.

"Something like that."

"Hey, little man," he holds his arms open for David. "That throwing arm looks amazing."

"Thanks, Dad." David doesn't hesitate running into Nathan's arms. A part of me questions his motives for being here, but seeing the pure joy on David's face is worth whatever it is. "I really hope I get to be quarterback."

"You will be." He lets go of David and puts his arms to the side. "How would you like to stay the night with me this weekend? We could throw the football and go to the movies."

"Mom, can I?" There's no way in hell I could tell that hopeful face no. Even if Nathan is up to something.

"Sure, we can swing by the house and get you some clothes."

"I can take him shopping for a few things tonight. It's not a big deal. He needs some clothes for my house anyway." Yeah, he's got a hidden agenda, but I won't let this come between David's relationship with him. Regardless if I date, he still needs his father in his life.

"Okay." I bend down and give David a big hug. "Change out of your cleats and give me your water bottle. I'll take them home and get them cleaned up."

"Thanks, Mom." He slides the shoes off and puts his sandals on.

"I'll see you Saturday night."

"It may be Sunday," Nathan interrupts. "I might take him to see my parents."

Yeah, the ones who never call and ask about him. "Okay, sounds good. Just keep me updated." I wrap David in one more hug. "I love you. Have fun."

"I love you, too." It hurts like hell to see him walk away with his dad, but he needs this. If only it were more often than when it's convenient for Nathan.

Now I have an entire weekend to myself. Whatever am I going to do?

* * *

My car leads me straight to Out of the Ashes. Should I have gone home? Probably. I didn't really want to, though. The grin on Carlos's face when he sees me walk through the doors makes my decision more than worth it.

I spot someone paying their tab at the bar and I wait patiently behind them to grab their stool. Once they are done, I slide on top of the stool and before I can sit all the way up, a beer is sitting in front of me. The man I'm dating smiling down at me. The line has already blurred from fake to real. At least, it has for me. Maybe I'm rusty after so many years out of the game. I don't want to think I'll glom onto the first man who shows kindness to both my son and I, but it feels like it could be something with him.

"Where's David?" Carlos leans on the bar, his sole focus on me and not the patrons lining the bar top.

"Oh, uh, Nathan said he was going to keep him for the weekend and take him to see his other grandparents."

He taps the bar with his knuckles. "So, you have the entire weekend free?"

My cheeks warm, and I hope they aren't turning bright red. "Yes."

"I can probably get out of here a little early." He glances around. The bar is busy, but not like I've seen it before football season. Friday nights in a small town means most people will be at the game. They may get swamped afterward, but that will depend on the results.

"You don't have to do that." I take a sip of my beer. "I just wanted to let you know."

"I see," he pauses for a second, "you could have texted me to tell me."

"Probably. But I wanted to see your reaction." Another sip. "Oh, and I figured out how we should do our grilling challenge. Either this Sunday, or next, we can have your family and mine at my house. I'll turn on the game and we can make a day of it."

"Are you ready for our families to meet?"

Shrugging my shoulders, I lean forward. "I mean, most of my family knows who you are already. It's not like they don't come to this bar."

"True enough." He nods, taking the information in. "I'll get with my mom and see what she has planned. Until then, why don't you go home and get ready."

"For what?"

"Dinner."

"But, aren't you working?"

He glances around the bar and looks toward Eric. "Yeah, but Eric knows he may be up for a promotion. This will be a good time to see if he can handle things on his own. We've given him easy shifts before this."

"Okay." I finish my beer. "If anything changes, let me know. I'm fine with waiting until tomorrow."

"I'm not." He smirks, and I can't help but wonder what sort of trouble I have coming my way.

I stand on the legs of the stool, lean over the bar and place a chaste kiss on his lips. "I guess I'll see you in a bit. Let me know if anything changes."

"I will." He watches me get off the stool and I can feel his eyes on me as I walk toward the door.

Once I'm outside, I glance down. I'm going to need to do more than change. A shower is in order after sweating on the side of the football field. A part of me feels like something that could blow up in my face is going to happen, but I'm not going to focus on that. Instead, I'll focus on the man who's been amazing to me the past couple of weeks. I never thought I'd be the type of person who would fall fast, but being with Carlos is testing that theory.

22

carlos

CAROLINE HASN'T BEEN GONE two minutes, and I'm already searching for Eric. I hope like hell he can cover me. Her having an entirely free weekend feels like a Godsend. Even though, I feel like her ex is only taking their son for the weekend for something nefarious.

I didn't miss the look he was giving me when David told me bye at practice. Honestly, I don't know what Caroline even saw in him. That's three interactions I've had with the man, and he has a douchebag neon sign blinking over his head. Most people would say I feel this way because I'm dating his ex-wife, but it's more than that. They are completely opposite people. Caroline is kind-hearted and values her family. The only thing I see Nathan value is what benefits himself.

Finally, I see Eric make his way back to the bar. Took him long enough. "Hey, you got a minute?"

"Sure, whatcha need?" He eyes me before I can even ask. "This has something to do with your girl, doesn't it?"

Geez, am I that easy to read? "Yeah, she unexpectedly has the weekend to herself, and I kind of want to take her to dinner tonight. And maybe switch shifts with you tomorrow?"

Eric taps his finger on his chin, thinking it over. Though I think he's purposefully keeping me on edge. "I don't know, Man. You're gone more than you're here these days."

Damn it. I knew asking him was going to be risky. I've been expecting too much of him. And he's right. I've been leaving work more often than not to spend time with Caroline. That might make me a shitty boss and co-owner. "I get it."

Eric holds up a finger to silence me, "You didn't let me finish. But I'll do it for you."

"Wh-what?"

"Look, this is the happiest I've seen you in a long time. And it's not like you haven't worked from open until close a million times." He shrugs as if he has no choice, "I'll do it for you. Go out and woo your girl. My mom was a single parent. I know how hard those free weekends are to come by."

I wrap him in a quick hug and let him go. "Thanks. I owe you."

"When did you become a hugger? I don't think I like it." He laughs and continues his way behind the bar. This kid... here lately, I don't know what I'd do without him, but I'm glad to have him in my corner. I won't leave just yet. I want to give Caroline time to get ready. I just know the next thirty minutes are going to drag, and all I can think about is her. And how often she's had someone bend to her every will. This may have been fake for her in the beginning, but for me...it's always been real.

* * *

My phone dings with a text as I pull into Caroline's driveway.

Caroline: I'm ready whenever you are

Relief floods through me. I'm not here to early. Waiting to leave work and stopping by the house to change give her extra time. I even managed to stop by the store and pick up her favorite beer. It's sitting in my fridge cooling. It may be presumptuous for me to think she's going to come home with me, but I'm hopeful she will. I'd like her to see where I live, amongst other things.

Rather than replying, I get out of the car and make my way up the porch steps. I knock, one, two, three times and wait for her to answer. When she does, I swear I stop breathing. "You look amazing."

She's wearing a short, strapless black dress that hugs her curves in all the right places. She looks great in yoga pants, but they don't do her body justice at all.

Pulling up the top of her dress, a sheepish smile tugs at her lips. "Thank you. I wasn't sure if it was too much or not enough since I don't know where we're going."

After seeing her, I'm not sure I want to go anywhere. The need to keep what's mine hidden from everyone else is simmering just under the surface. "I vote we stay in."

"Nope." She holds up a hand. "I put on real clothes, we're going out."

Point made. "Can I come in?"

She purses her lips, and takes me in from head to toe. "If you come in, we may never leave. Let me grab my purse."

I chuckle and shake my head. Smart woman. Other than spending time with her, my new goal now includes peeling that dress off her body, inch by inch.

Caroline comes back with a small bag over her shoulder

and slides her phone into a pocket. She closes and locks the door behind her. I hold my arm out in presentation. "Your chariot awaits."

I slide my hand into hers and lead her to the passenger side of the car. Opening the door, I wait until she's in and close it behind her. I know we've met for breakfast here and there, and the one time we had dinner in, but this feels like a true first date. Our debut into the world announcing we are a bona fide couple.

She's quiet as we pull out of the driveway and head back into town. I want to ask her if everything is okay, but she'll let me know on her own terms. My hand is on her thigh, and I give it a small squeeze, letting her know I'm there.

She puts one of her hands on top and leans her head on my shoulder. "Do you think we're moving too fast?"

That's a turn I wasn't expecting this to take. "I don't think so. Why?"

She sighs, "I don't know. It just feels like whatever we have is too good to be true. Even if it started out as fake, I can't ignore the feelings I have for you. Hell, I had a crush on you before any of this even happened."

"You did?" I suspected, but I didn't want to assume. It was hard to miss the glances she always shot me, and how she would come to the bar to order her own drink even when she was with her friends. A part of me always hoped I was the reason, but another part thought it was also because her friends always got her cocktails instead of the beer she drinks when she comes in. Unless, they were setting this whole thing up. After spending a day with them, I know they are capable of it.

"Yeah."

"Then why were you going to say no when I asked you out?"

"I don't know." Another shrug. "I didn't think I deserved being in a relationship. The last one I had didn't turn out so great. I couldn't keep him happy enough to stay. And since then, I put all of myself into raising David."

The urge to slam on my brakes in the middle of this deserted road is hard to resist. Not because what she said makes me angry, but because she should know none of those things are true. "Caroline, you deserve every ounce of happiness that comes your way. Hopefully, I'm a part of that. But even if I'm not, don't ever question what you deserve. You are an amazing mother, daughter, and friend. How your ex treated you, and made you feel, that's on him. Don't let his actions frame the rest of your life."

I feel her lift her head up. A quick glance in her direction, and her focus is on me. "You are the only person who has told me something along those lines outside of my family and friends."

"Honestly, nobody else's opinion should matter. Especially your ex-husband's. If he can't handle his loss of an amazing woman, that's his problem."

"You might be my favorite person right now." I hear the smile in her voice.

"I'm trying to be your favorite person ever." As soon as I say it, I know it sounds ridiculous. Her favorite person should and will always be David. I would never make her choose between her son and myself. What kind of asshole would that make me?

"You're working your way up the list." She pulls her phone out of her bag, checking for messages before she places it back inside. "So, where are we eating? I'm starving."

* * *

It almost would have been worth it to stay in. The looks and whispered secrets by some of the patrons were almost too much to bear. There's no doubt in my mind it was about me and Caroline. It was like the moment we entered, everyone decided they wanted to give input about us. Never to our faces, but with mouths covered by their hands and quick, curious glances in our direction.

I get it to some extent. Even though I've lived here for a while, Caroline has lived here her entire life. Of course, there is going to be scrutiny. I tried, unsuccessfully, to prepare for whatever might come our way, but misjudged how shitty some people are. Never mind the fact I've served a lot of these people on multiple occasions at the bar. It's like she's not allowed to date after a failed marriage, and it's such bullshit. They could have been staring at us for other reasons, but I refuse to believe a majority of our town thinks we shouldn't be together for any other reason. If that were the case, I'd have to not serve them next time they come into the bar.

Caroline must feel the tension running off me as we walk out of the restaurant and judgmental stares. "Ignore them. They are assholes that refuse to believe the world has changed instead of being whatever the hell they want it to be."

"That isn't what bothered me. It was the way they looked at you. As if you're some person that needs to be pitied."

"You realize none of that matters to me, right? I haven't cared what other people think of me in years, and I don't intend to start now."

The strength of this woman never ceases to amaze me. The world could be on fire, and she'll dust herself off to continue doing what needs to be done. "Which is why you are a much better person than me."

I open the car door and wait until she's inside before closing the door and getting in on my side. "Where to now?"

"That's up to you." I turn on the car, but don't make a

move to put it in gear. "Are you ready to go home? I can drop you off, or we can get ice cream and head back to my place."

"Definitely ice cream."

I put the car in gear and leave the parking lot, elated she doesn't want to go home just yet. Who knows...maybe she won't go home at all tonight.

23

caroline

THE PROTECTIVENESS CARLOS has over me is sweet, though unnecessary. When Nathan left, I had to grow a thick skin. Rumors flew all over this town and it almost destroyed me. My mom was the only strength I had, other than David.

Either way, I'm happy he feels the need to protect me. It's something I've never felt before outside of my family. He's the person who makes me feel safe. He makes me feel like I can take on the world. "How did you know that was my favorite ice cream shop?"

He looks over at me and grins as he's driving through town. "Probably because it's the only place in town. It's not like we have many options."

"True." He turns down a road I've been on a million times. "But what if I liked fast food ice cream."

"Nobody actually likes that."

"I'm positive someone out there does." I hold out his ice cream cone putting it close enough to his mouth that he can take a bite without his eyes leaving the road. "In fact, David is rather fond of soft serve."

"Thanks," he mutters around his bite. "Fine, I'll quit bagging on soft serve."

Taking another bite of my ice cream, I watch the road. My foot taps to the beat of the music coming through the speakers. It's not on beat in the slightest, but I hope he doesn't notice the nerves for what they are. I'm about to enter his domain. He's been in mine, and I felt comfortable because we were in my space. Now...I don't know what to expect.

I lift the ice cream cone to him again, but he shakes his head. "We're almost there."

Another block down and he pulls into a driveway. The house looks average size from the outside. Not too big or small. "Is this it?"

"Yep." He turns off the car, gets out, and comes around to my side of the car, opening the door. "Let me take that."

He grabs his cone out of my hand and helps me out of the car. I stand, grab my purse and move out of the way of the door before closing it behind me. I fidget with the bottom of my dress, pulling it down until it covers almost my entire thigh.

Carlos leads me to the door, and we're there a few minutes as he finds the key he's looking for. I take a bite of my ice cream while waiting. I don't know what else to do. It's one of those moments where you don't know what to do with your hands.

Finally, he opens the door and pushes it wide before motioning me inside. "Welcome to my humble abode."

He flicks a light switch on, and I take in the front room. The door opens straight into the living room. The kitchen is at the back, and there's a short hallway that veers off to the right. I'm assuming that's where the bedroom is located. Not that

I'm thinking about going to the bedroom. Well, not right now anyway.

The thing that surprises me are all the pictures hanging on the walls. I walk further into the living room and my eyes find the collage of frames behind the couch. I see his mom and sisters. There's also a man in a few of them. I can only guess that is his dad, despite how little he talks about him. "Wow, I bet your sisters feel famous with the number of photos you have of them."

"Pictures are pretty much my only decoration. Every time I felt like I wasn't going anywhere, looking at them gave me strength." He closes the door and walks over to me. "Plus, this is the only way I can look at them without them insulting me about something."

"They aren't that bad." I take another bite of my ice cream, trying to finish it before it melts more than it has.

"That's because you don't know them," he laughs, "last weekend was them on good behavior. They're ten times worse when nobody's watching."

"I'm not sure how I feel about that." I lean closer to the wall to study the pictures of him and his sisters as they've grown up. Their dad with them until about five years ago, from what I can guess. "Does that mean they will start picking on me as much as they do you when they are comfortable around me?"

He shakes his head, "Doubt it. They like you. You and David have quickly become their favorites."

"Good to know." I finish my ice cream and continue my perusal of his house. Other than the pictures there isn't a lot of decoration. The only thing visible are a few books on a shelf. Curiosity gets the best of me and I bend down to see what he's been reading. "So, you like dragons?"

"More like fantasy in general, but yes, dragons for the

most part. I mean, who wouldn't want a freaking dragon? They're badass. They breathe fire and destroy lands."

"Yes, dragons are pretty cool. The ending to that show sucked, though."

"Wait, you watch the show?" I turn to see what exactly his facial expression is and why he'd be surprised I watch it. And I'm right his eyebrows are raised and his mouth is wide open.

"Why wouldn't I?"

"I don't know. You have witch books, and watch vampire stuff. So, I kind of assumed that was your thing."

I cross my arms over my chest and glare at him. "I can be multifaceted. Just because I like vampires, doesn't mean I don't like dragons or dire wolves or anything like that."

"Okay." He's smart not to say anything else. "I take back what I said earlier. As soon as my sisters find out you're into fantasy stuff. They're going to pick on you, too."

"They can bring it. I'm not ashamed of my fandoms." I'm not exactly sure what to do from here, though. He also isn't offering any sort of direction. "So, what do we do now?"

"Well, I could show you the bedroom. Or, we can watch a movie." He looks down at the ground as if the bedroom comment wasn't supposed to come out.

Gotta love when those inside thoughts become outside thoughts. "I think I like the bedroom idea." I clasp my hands behind my back and sway back and forth on my feet. Honestly, I'm willing to do anything to get out of these damn heels.

"Are you sure?"

He lifts his head and looks at me. "Let's not pretend that's not where we're going to end up anyway."

"Well, I mean, I kind of hoped, but I didn't want to presume."

"Presume away." He walks over to me and grabs my hand before leading me to his room. It feels weird and normal, all at the same time. Like we have lived this exact moment a thousand times while also being the first time we've ever gone down this road.

His room is just as empty as the rest of his house. An alarm clock, sits on the nightstand with a few chargers hanging over the edge. A long dresser fills the space along one wall and a tall dresser sits just inside the door.

His bed though? That's massive. If I had to guess, it's probably a California king. Definitely bigger than mine. Also, way bigger than the couch.

Opposite of his bed is a TV attached to the wall. I'm not sure if he spends a lot of his time in here or in the living room. But if I had to guess, he mostly uses this space as a place to sleep with the hours that he puts in at the bar. This is a small peek into the life of the man I'm falling for, and I'm grateful he's showing it to me. He doesn't need a lot of things, and the value he places on family means a lot since my family is also incredibly important to me.

He leads me toward the bed and sets me down on the black and red bedspread. "Let me help you out of those shoes. They can't be comfortable."

"Those might be my favorite words I've heard today. I don't even think I've worn these shoes in years because of how badly they hurt my feet."

"Then why did you wear them tonight?"

"Because they make my legs look good and this dress does not call for regular shoes."

"Honestly, I hear the floor calling your dress."

I can't help the giggle that escapes my lips. "Pickup lines aren't really your thing, are they?"

"What was your first clue?"

"It's just an observation. You don't have to feel alone in that because they're not mine either. The only thing I managed to do when I thought someone was attractive is turn them down for a date and then announce them as my boyfriend."

Carlos laughs as he pulls the straps from around my ankle and slides my shoes off my feet. "Hey, it worked. Otherwise, we wouldn't be here."

"No, if we were still fake dating we wouldn't be here. But somewhere along the lines you've managed to make me feel real things."

"Is that so bad?"

"Not really. Just..." I pause to figure out the right word, "unexpected."

Carlos takes his shoes off before standing over me. "Okay, but so is the fact you're in my bed, and still in that dress."

My cheeks heat, and I lean back on my elbows, "We could always do something about that."

"That we can." He reaches for my hands and I sit up, placing mine in his. Curious as to what he's going to do.

Once I'm standing, he takes a step back. His gaze roving over every inch of my body. In all honesty, it makes me want to squirm. But, I won't. I also like it. Nobody has ever looked at me the way he is right now. As if I'm his everything and just plain his.

Done with his admiration, he takes a step closer again. And another until he's directly in front of me. I look up to meet his eyes and am taken aback by the desire I see. He lifts a hand and traces it over my shoulder, and does the same with the other. A shiver of anticipation runs through my body.

His lips brush against my jawline, while his fingers move across my body. They graze the top edge of my dress and start pulling it down. Slowly, as if I'm a present he must carefully unwrap.

His mouth follows the dress's dissent. Kissing every inch of skin now visible. He bends as he pulls the dress down. Small kisses down my stomach, and I feel like I'm baring my soul to him.

My insecurities over my body since having David creep into my thoughts. My stomach isn't as flat as it used to be and stretch marks are visible where they didn't used to be. It's why I left my shirt on that night at my house. I didn't want him to see what my body truly looks like.

I take in a breath and he notices, pausing his exploration. "Are you okay?"

"Yeah." I swallow past the lump in my throat. "I just... don't look the same as I did before having kids. Other than my ex, you're the only person who has seen me."

He removes my dress the rest of the way, and I step out of it before he tosses it aside. He walks me back to the bed, until I'm sitting again. "Never be ashamed of your body." He pulls the strapless bra I'm wearing over my head and throws it behind him.

I lie back and close my eyes, "But you do—"

My panties are pulled off before I can finish. I hear a drawer open and close before foil is ripped open. At least he's prepared. A moment later I can feel him hovering over me.

"Look at me." His thumb traces a line along my cheek. I open my eyes and all his attention is on me. "You. Are. Beautiful. Any asshole who has told you otherwise, is just that...an asshole."

His arms are on either side of my head and I can't help but notice the way he's looking at me. He means every word he says. I don't detect a hint of deceit. "You mean that?"

He bends down and places a kiss on the corner of my mouth. "Why would I lie?"

I shift my head until my lips meet his, and wrap my arms around his neck. That's all the answer he needs. He deepens the kiss while positioning himself between my legs.

The wait is torture. I hook my legs around his waist, guide

him into me. He repositions himself on his elbow and wraps one arm around me, bringing us closer.

Our bodies move in sync as we get lost in each other. It's not rushed and rampant like the last time. We take our time, enjoying every minute. I feel safe and taken care of when I'm with him. If I wanted him to stop right now, I know he would without question.

The pressure is building and I roll my hips. As much as I don't want this to end right now, I need the release. I pull him closer to me, my tongue darting into his mouth. My hips roll faster, and he pulls his arm out from around me. He reaches between us, his thumb circling my clit while he thrusts. It's exactly the friction I need, and before long I'm yelling his name and seeing stars behind my closed lids.

24

carlos

MY WEEKEND with Caroline has flown by. Today we have our combined family cookout, and I don't want to leave our personal paradise we've created. We haven't even left the house. Angie text me yesterday saying she didn't need me to come in, and that's a gift horse I wasn't going to look in the mouth.

"Do you need me to help with anything?" Caroline asks from where she's sitting on the counter. She is wearing my shirt, and I never understood the appeal of seeing your girl in your clothes until now.

"Nope. I've got it." I'm frying some potatoes to mix with the eggs. "After we eat, we can run by your place so you can change."

"What are we doing after that?"

"Going to the grocery store. We need supplies for this epic grilling challenge."

"Oh," she gasps. "I completely forgot about that."

"So, the sex is that good, huh?" I grin even though she can't see me. "Does that mean you concede?"

"Hell no." I hear her feet hit the ground after hopping off the counter. Her arms come around my waist and she leans against me. "You're going down."

"You have a funny way of showing it."

"What? I can't sweeten up to the competition."

I turn off the burner under the potatoes, and pour them into the egg mixture. I grab the tortillas Mom sent home with me from the fridge and set them next to the stove. "That's not going to work. It takes a lot more than a hug to make me back down."

She starts tugging at my pants, and I put my hand over hers. "I'm going to burn breakfast."

"Let it burn." She moves until she's between me and the stove.

I pull her away, lift her up and set her back on the counter. "You're not going to tempt me so easily." I move between her legs and run my hands up her thighs, relishing the shiver that passes through her body. "Besides, we're running out of time. Our families will be at your place in a couple of hours and we don't have anything to cook."

Her hand trails a path down my chest, stopping at the edge of my sweats yet again. "Fine. But remember, you could have this. Instead, you're being lame and making breakfast."

"Pouting will get you nowhere." I give her a quick peck and return to my cooking.

"If you say so." She watches as I finish breakfast, but doesn't say another word. Or try to seduce me again. Maybe I am a dumbass for not taking her up on it.

* * *

My mom and sisters are late as usual. I'm almost certain it's because my sisters changed five thousand times before settling on an outfit. Luckily, I don't feel nervous around her family since I've seen them all at the bar at some point. The only person missing is David, and I have a feeling his dad is bringing him home late on purpose.

"Why pork chops?" Reaf leans against the counter in his sister's house. We had it here because there is plenty of room in the backyard for the kids to run around.

I shrug, "I don't know. It's what your sister picked."

"Because that's the one thing she grills really well. She totally set you up." He laughs and takes a drink of his beer.

"She told me she was a grilling master."

He laughs and claps his hand against the surface. "She's full of shit. Anything else she burns, or doesn't cook all the way."

"Language, Reaf." I hear his wife scold him from the living room. "Between you and our friends Layla will be running around shouting f bombs."

"You're not exactly a saint," he calls back. He turns back toward me, "When we first met it was pretty much her favorite word."

These two crack me up, and it's no wonder they work so well together. They feed off each other, and remind me of stories of my own parents. That is what I'm hoping happens with me and Caroline. "Any advice you can give me about how she cooks them?"

"Oh, no," he lifts his hands up. "I'm not getting between this battle. She'll forgive you, if you beat her. But me? She'll come after me for giving you a heads up. She's older and scarier."

I've never seen that side of her, but I'll take his word for it. After all, he's her brother and knows her better than I ever could. "I guess I better get started on my seasoning while she's not paying attention to me. Has she said when David is supposed to be home?"

He shakes his head. "All I know is Nathan was supposed to drop him off an hour ago, and he still hasn't shown up. I'm sure he'll be here soon."

"Yeah." I turn toward the counter and look through everything I bought at the store. Pushing some items away while bringing some forward. I'm not the greatest cook, I'll admit that, but I've learned a thing or two from my mom when it comes to cooking.

A car pulls into the driveway and I want nothing more than to rush to the door to see who it is. There are only two possible options since everyone is already here. It's not my place, though. This is Caroline's house, not mine. I'm not sure why I'm so anxious. Most of it has to be because of Nathan. While I don't think he'll make a scene in front of a crowd, I can't be sure. The last thing I want is for Caroline to be stressed because of his bullshit.

My fears are unwarranted. As soon as the door opens, I hear my sisters asking for David and groaning as they are told he's not here yet. Caroline introduces my family to hers, and it feels nice to know there aren't any problems.

"Hi, Mijo." My mom sets a round, foil covered package on the counter beside me before giving me a hug. "What are you cooking?"

"Chops." I nod toward the pans where they are evenly split. "Apparently it's Caroline's specialty."

"Who told you that?" the woman in question asks, voice high pitched.

"A little bird."

"I'm going to murder Reaf for spilling my secrets." Well, he was right about one thing. And the fact she knew it was him right off the bat tells me he's ratted her out more than once.

"At least now I know your siblings annoy you as much as mine annoy me."

My mom smacks me on the arm, "Be nice to your sisters."

"Fine," I grumble. "So, is the grill ready to go?"

Caroline puts her hands on her hips and eyes me. "It is. I was hoping David would already be home, though."

"Why don't you call him?" It sucks he isn't here yet and I hope like hell her ex isn't doing it on purpose. "I'll work on the salad so it'll be ready before we go outside."

"Okay." She worries her bottom lip and walks out of the kitchen, through the living room, and disappears down the hallway.

"Be gentle with her. It must be hard talking to an ex."

"I know, and he doesn't make it easy. I just don't know if I should step in and help." I grab the lettuce and begin chopping it.

"Not until she says it's okay." She pats my arm and walks toward the living room. "Also, don't touch those." She points toward the foil package. "I brought them for David."

"You don't bring me homemade tortillas anymore."

"Because you're grown and you know how to make them. You're just too lazy to do it."

She's not wrong. It's such a pain in the ass, and not my favorite thing in the world. The results are worth it, though. "True."

"Do you need me to do anything?"

"No, you go visit. I'm going to finish up here and see if Caroline needs me to do anything else."

It doesn't take me long to finish the salad. Caroline still hasn't come out of the hallway, and I'm worried something may have happened. I make my way to where I last saw her. She's standing in the middle of what I assume is her room, her voice an angry whisper. "He was supposed to be home two hours ago."

She pauses to hear whatever he has to say. "If he isn't home in the next thirty minutes, I'll get the cops involved." He must say something, but she cuts him off. "I don't care, Nathan. This is what happens every time he stays with you. The time is in our divorce papers. And I don't care if you threaten to take me to court. I can guarantee I won't make it easy."

She turns and sees me standing there. I mouth, "Are you okay?"

She nods and listens to more of what Nathan has to say. "Thirty minutes. I'm not playing." She hangs up before throwing the phone on her bed. "I swear he has been put here to drive me insane. He's lost his mind if he thinks he can take me to court and win. I've been documenting all the times he hasn't shown up."

My strides are long as I approach her and wrap her in my arms. "David will be here soon, then we get on with our challenge."

"Thanks."

I kiss the top of her head. "You know you don't have to go through all the crap with Nathan alone, right? Your family is there to support you, and I'm not going anywhere."

"You say that now, but you haven't witnessed my ex-douchebag in the midst of a temper tantrum."

I let her go and meet her eyes. "And he hasn't seen what a strong united front looks like."

She lifts up on her toes and kisses my cheek. "This is why you are amazing." Grabbing my hand, she leads me toward the door. "If I know Nathan, he'll haul ass over here with David to avoid ruining his reputation. Why don't you go check the grill so we can get started as soon as he gets here?"

* * *

It's time for the big reveal. My pork chops against Caroline's. Both look, and smell, delicious. Hopefully I get this win, especially after she was right about when David would be home. The only shitty part about the situation is she wouldn't let me or Reaf meet Nathan up front. He was about as happy about it as I was.

"Judging this is going to be hard," Caroline's mom says. "Both look amazing."

"It won't be hard for me," Marisol grins. "I'm choosing Caroline by default."

"That's not fair." It comes out whiny, but it's not. "You have to try the food before you decide who wins."

"He's right, my love." Mom pats her shoulder.

Bryce looks over both sets of chops and sighs. "The only way this is going to be somewhat fair, since we know who made each one, is if y'all wait outside while we taste test."

I glance over at Caroline and she nods. "Okay, we'll be on the porch." I motion for her to go ahead of me, and we walk out.

"I can't believe they're kicking me out of my own kitchen." Caroline sits in one of the chairs.

"Not all of them." I sit down next to her. "Just your baby brother. At least they didn't automatically vote against you."

"That's because I'm the favorite." She grins. "And thanks for the pep talk earlier. Things will work out. Last time he pulled a stunt like this, he disappeared from David's life for a while. I just get so sick of making excuses for him. And tired of holding my tongue around David, even though it's the right thing to do."

"You're a lot stronger than me. I would have lost my shit on him a long time ago."

"My mom was a good role model. Our dad bailed on us when Bryce was a toddler. Even to this day she never says anything bad about him. She told me we'd figure out how we felt about him as we got older."

"And did you?"

"Yep. He never tried to see us. No cards, or calls, for our birthdays. I knew he was a piece of crap, and I never felt like I missed out on anything. I was hoping it would be different for David, but so far...it's more of the same."

"Not to sound like your mom, but he'll figure it out."

"I know," she sighs and leans against me, "waiting for him to do that is harder than I thought possible. Now I know what my mom went through."

Before I can say anything, the front door opens and Reaf sticks his head out. "We're ready."

We're barely through the door when Marisol yells, "Caroline is the winner."

"Seriously?" I lift my hands in the air.

"Mijo, you used too much red pepper. We could barely eat it."

Gabi rolls her eyes. "I could handle it, but everyone else couldn't."

"That's fair." I grab Caroline's hand and lift it to my lips. "Congrats on the win."

"Thank you." She curtsies. "Now, let's eat. I'm starving."

I think we all are. Dinner was pushed so we could wait on David. All of us descend on the food. My pork chops are pushed to the side in favor of Caroline's. I take a bite of hers and they were right. It's delicious. Clearly, I should stick to pouring drinks. Cooking is not my strong point.

25

caroline

IT'S BEEN weeks and as I suspected we haven't heard a peep from Nathan. He likes to parade David around like he's father of the year, and he can't be bothered to show up for his son when he doesn't gain anything from it.

He even stopped coming to football practice. It sucks seeing David look for him in the stands. And it hurts thinking he'll get used to it, and no longer look. His dad isn't the only person he tries to find in the crowd of parents. He scans for Carlos, too.

That disappointment doesn't hit him as hard, though. Carlos is honest with him about when he'll be there. He doesn't make promises he can't keep.

"Mom, can we see Carlos tonight?" David helps me load his football gear into the backseat.

"He's working tonight, but maybe we can meet up for breakfast?"

"Ooo, I want waffles." He jumps up and down.

It's adorable that food makes him happy because...same.

"I'll call him later and see if he's up for it. But for now, why don't we grab something to eat then watch a movie."

"As long as I get to pick. I'm not watching your vampire movies." It's like he's not even my kid.

"What's wrong with them?"

"There's too much kissing." He makes a noise like he's about to puke. "I don't want to watch movies about love. Let's watch a superhero movie."

He's just like, that kid in The Princess Bride. Little does he realize almost all of his favorite hero movies also have a romance plot. He just doesn't know it...yet.

"You can't stay up all night, though. Especially if we're getting up to go to breakfast, and we have to get all your stuff ready for your game."

He fist pumps the air, "Yes, we're going to win."

"Now you sound like your Uncle Bryce."

"Hopefully, him and Carlos come to see me as quarterback."

"They are."

"For real?" He bounces around in the backseat.

"Yes," I laugh at his excitement. "Carlos is working the late shift and your uncle is driving down from school. He wants to see his star quarterback."

I can feel the happiness emanating off him, and even if his dad isn't around to give him that joy, I'm glad he has people that make him feel that way.

We pull up to the closest fast-food place. I grab him a kid's meal and me a burger. Within minutes we're back on the road. David is already digging into his food, and I don't blame him. After all the running they do up and down the field, I'd be hungry, too.

David hops out of the car before I can put it in park. "Don't forget your trash," I yell after him. He comes back with less pep in his step and grabs the bag.

"Can I take a shower before we watch the movie?"

"Sure thing, kiddo." He grabs the house key from me and lets himself in. Which leaves me to carry his gear inside. All of this is going straight to the washer. I can smell it at arm's length. There's one thing I don't miss about boys playing sports, and it's the stench.

My phone rings as I'm opening the door, and I pull it out of my back pocket. "Hello?"

"Hey, Care." Emily's panicked voice comes over the line. "You got a minute?"

"Sure." I push the door closed behind me and throw his clothes into the washer. "What's up?"

"Any chance you can come in tomorrow?"

"If it were any other day, I would, but it's David's first game." I feel horrible saying I can't, but I can't miss this one. "What happened?"

"Sam is out of town, and I can't get ahold of Kate. A call came in about fifteen minutes ago for an emergency flower order for a quinceñera. The original florist screwed up their order and they need it for tomorrow night."

"How many arrangements?"

"Two dozen."

"If I come in the morning, do you think we can knock it out?" David is going to be upset about not having breakfast with Carlos, but sometimes things come up. And this is my job. It's a rarity I even get weekends off. "And would you be able to deliver them all?"

She doesn't say anything for a few moments and I worry I've made her mad for not being able to help with that part. "Yeah, that should work. Want to meet at the shop at seven?"

"That works." Now to let down the two most important guys in my life. "I'll see you then."

David comes out of his room with his clothes, headed for the bathroom. "What's wrong?"

"Bad news, kiddo."

He cocks his head to the side, confused with a touch of concern. "Are you okay?"

"Yeah, but we might have to reschedule breakfast. Emily needs my help at the shop because Sam and Kate aren't here."

His shoulders slump and I feel awful. "It's okay, Mom. Breakfast can wait. Maybe I can help you and we can finish faster."

"That would be great." My sweet boy. Always willing to help out when he doesn't have to.

"Eat before your food gets cold," he grins, "and then it's superhero time."

He goes into the bathroom and closes the door. The water runs, and I know he'll take a quick shower. I unwrap my burger and sit on the couch.

David doesn't know that Carlos and I planned breakfast before I even suggested it. I need to let him know about the change of plans.

Caroline: We'll have to raincheck on breakfast. Emily needs my help at the shop.

I'm not sure when he'll be able to respond. The high school game is out of town and the bar is sure to be busy. I just hope he isn't as upset about the news as David was. The two of them are bonding in a way I never could have imagined, and I hope like hell things work out between me and Carlos. If it doesn't, I'm not the only one who will be heartbroken.

* * *

"David, can you hand me that string and paper?" Emily calls over her shoulder while I bring another bunch of flowers to our work area.

"Yes, ma'am." He grabs the items and sets them down. "Can I help with anything?"

I set the flowers down to arrange them. "I know it's early, but why don't you keep an eye on the front of the store to see if anyone comes in. You can take my phone and play some games."

"Okay." His face lights up and he grabs my phone before going to the front.

"Nice way to distract him," Emily laughs, "you'd think the kid never gets to play games."

I shrug and lay the different types of flowers out in groups. "He doesn't get a lot of time on my phone. He plays some games on the system Reaf gave him, but I limit his time on it."

"Smart."

"I have my moments."

She grabs her phone and puts on some music while we work. It's not too loud so we can hear David, but we can still hear it. We work in silence for a few minutes. Each of us grabbing the flowers we need to arrange temporary bouquets until she can get them to the venue to place in the table vases.

"Are you sure you can get this delivered and set up by yourself?" Guilt is gnawing at me even though Kate is missing in action. I tried calling her, but it went straight to voicemail. It's not fair to ask Emily to do this on her own.

"Yeah." She continues working on her bouquet. "It may take a little longer, but that's what happens with last minute orders. I sold them at a hell of an upcharge to cover our time. It'd be nice if Kate answered her phone though."

"Well, let me know what time you head over to the banquet hall. If it's before the game starts, I'll come help you." I'm going to stop by Kate's house on the way to the game, also. It's unlike her to not answer her phone. It's usually glued to her hands.

"Thanks. I think I'll be fine, though."

"If you're sure..." She's the quietest amongst our little group, and usually does whatever the rest of us do. I don't want her to feel like she's carrying this burden on her own because I know she won't speak up.

"Mom!" David yells from the front. I can't tell if he's scared or excited. I jump up and over the flowers, rushing to see what caused his outburst.

"What is it?" It takes me a moment to find him, and he's by the front door. He's not alone, though. Standing next to him...is Carlos. "Wh–, what are you doing here?"

He holds plastic sacks up in his hands. "You couldn't make it for breakfast, so I brought it to you. I hope Emily likes waffles."

"I love them," she yells from the back room. How in the world did she even hear him?

"You didn't have to do that." I swear he surprises me in the best ways.

He walks forward, David by his side, and sets the bags on the counter. "I know. I might have also wanted to see y'all."

"It's because he likes me best," David pipes in while rounding the counter to sit in the chair.

Carlos winks at me, "It sure is. Are you ready for your game this afternoon?" He pulls the meals out of the bags and sets them down.

David grabs one of the boxes and pops it open. "Definitely, we're totally going to win."

Shaking his head, Carlos hands me a box. "Don't be over-confident. The only thing you can do is go out there and play your best."

My son takes a bite of his waffle, no syrup or butter, just the waffle. He definitely didn't get that from me. "I can do that."

"Good deal." He points to the bottom of the bag, "The syrup and butter is in there. Want me to get Emily?"

"Nope." Emily walks in. "Emily is right here. I just had to

finish the arrangement I was working on." She ruffles David's hair, "Is that waffle good?"

"The best."

"If I get these flowers unloaded in time, maybe I'll come by and watch you play."

"Really?" His mouth is full. When he notices my stern look, he swallows what's in his mouth before continuing. "That would be awesome. I'm going to have my own cheerleaders."

We get through our breakfasts quickly. There's nothing left in our boxes besides leftover syrup. Emily has gone back to the store room, and I'm cleaning up our mess. "Thank you for breakfast."

"Not a problem. I figured you might be hungry."

"You figured correctly." I give him a kiss on the lips before backing up. Even though David has seen us kiss, I don't like to do it too much in front of him. This is still newish for all of us. "I need to finish helping Emily before we go check on Kate and get ready for the game. You're still coming, right?"

David glances in our direction at the question, waiting for Carlos's response. "Yep. I'm picking up Marisol and Gabriella in an hour."

"They're coming, too?" His smile widens.

"Yep. They insisted on coming to cheer you on."

"Awesome."

If he didn't have a big head about their victory they haven't had yet, he does now. "Can you throw these in the big trash cans in the back?"

"Yes, ma'am." He grabs the bags and waves at Carlos, "I'll see you at the game."

"See you there, buddy." Carlos pulls me into his arms as soon as David is out of sight. "Anything else you need me to help with before the game?"

"I don't think so." I lean against his chest. Even on unexpected, rushed mornings like this, his mere presence gives me comfort. Makes me feel like I'm on steady ground.

"Have you heard from his dad?"

"Nope."

"As much as I don't like the guy, it'll be pretty shitty if he doesn't show up for his first game."

I shrug my shoulders, even though it's difficult in his grasp. "We'll see if he shows. But I'm not holding my breath."

"At least David will have an entire section of the bleachers shouting for him."

"That he will." I wiggle out of his hold. Not because I want to, but I have things that need to get done. "I need to go help Emily. I feel horrible that she has to do the delivery on her own."

"I can take David to the game if you need a little extra time."

"It's okay. I mentioned helping her deliver them, and she refused. At least it's not an order for a full wedding. It's only a quinceñera."

Carlos chuckles, "You've obviously never been to one. They are usually about the size of a wedding. But the main place to put decorations is on the tables."

"Oh." I didn't know that. Maybe I should let her know. "Well, that's all the person ordered, so I'm guessing what we have is enough. Luckily, they chose flowers we have in stock."

"Good deal." He kisses the top of my head. "I'll let you get back to work. If you need anything, let me know."

I will. "Be careful picking up your sisters." Those three words are on the tip of my tongue, but I don't say them. It's too soon. No matter how much I'm falling for this man.

"I will. See you in a few hours." He walks out the door, and it takes everything in me to turn around and get to work. I'd much rather be going with him.

26

carlos

MY SISTERS ARE DRIVING me insane. When they said they'd be ready in an hour...they meant three. I don't know why they had to do their makeup and hair to sit in the warm sun on some uncomfortable bleachers. It makes no sense to me. And now, we're running late.

I fire off a text to Caroline because I don't want her to think I'm standing them up. That's not the type of guy I am.

Carlos: Running late. Apparently, my sisters need five thousand hours to get ready.
Caroline: It's okay. We've saved you a spot.

Thank goodness she's understanding. I glance at the clock; we might make it before kickoff if we push the speed limit.

"Are you sure y'all are good with hanging out at my house tonight?" It's been a long time since they've done that. Since Dad was alive.

"Do you have Netflix?" Marisol asks.

"Yes."

"What about Disney?" Gabriella adds.

"Yes."

They both giggle, but it's Marisol who answers, "Then as long as we have food, we'll be fine. We're teenagers not toddlers."

I long for the days when they were. They didn't talk back. Well, not much. And they were easier to be around. This whole teen girl thing is something I've never had to endure in my own house. It's hard to know when they are being sincere, or assholes.

"After the game, we'll run by the store and get the two of you some snacks and food." My fridge isn't stocked because them staying overnight was a last minute decision. They practically bombarded me when they finished getting ready. I mean, who wants to hang out with their grown ass brother over their teenage friends? I should be grateful they think I'm cool enough to hang out with.

"Awesome," They say in unison. If you didn't know better, you'd think they are twins, but they are about a year and a half apart. I was already out of the house when both of them were born. Considering I wasn't around much, it's a wonder we're somewhat close.

"We'll be there in about fifteen minutes."

"That was fast," Gabriella says.

"I may have driven a bit above the speed limit." Not that it's something I like to admit. They'll be driving soon enough and I don't want them driving like that.

"I'm telling Mom." Marisol scoots to the middle seat in the back.

Shrugging, I laugh. "Then I'll tell her you got out of your seatbelt while the car is moving."

Marisol is cackling next to me in the front seat. "You're

grown and threatening to tell on your baby sister. That's hilarious."

"I'm sure you'll do something to make me snitch at some point." That shuts her up fast. The football field is finally in view. Luckily there isn't a huge crowd for the little league game, and I find a parking spot close to the bleachers.

The three of us climb out of the car, and I lock it once the doors are closed. I worry we're too late until I see Caroline and her family about half way up the bleachers. But they aren't the only ones. Nathan is sitting directly in front of her, and if I'm not mistaken, he's leaning back until he's almost touching her.

"Who's that douche?" Marisol nods in Caroline's area.

"David's dad."

She must hear the sneer in my voice, because she says, "That bad, huh?"

"Well, he's nothing like our dad, that's for sure." Caroline waves to me, thinking I can't see her. "Let's go be in the most awkward situation I've ever known."

"I can make it uncomfortable for him." Gabi grins up at me.

"No, Mom would lose her shit if she found out we were anything but polite." Both of them nod and follow me up the steps. I know I should be happy he's here for David. It'd be nice if he was more stable in his life, but I can't help this gut feeling I have about him. And it's not good.

Caroline scoots over making room for me and my sisters. Nathan sits up straighter now that he realizes I'm behind him. He turns toward me, "Nice to see you again."

"Likewise." The smirk on his face is proof he's lying. It also means he knows exactly what he was doing by being so close to Caroline. I've seen guys like him come into the bar time and time again. They'll do anything to get under the skin of who they see as competition.

Normally, I'm not a jealous guy, but I have to keep

reminding myself to keep my cool. I will not be the person who makes a scene at a kid's football game.

"I see your sisters made it in one piece. I guess there wasn't too much arguing?" She bumps into my side and holds out her hand for me to take.

I slide my hand into hers and laugh. "Not too much. But they are staying the night at my place so things could get interesting."

"Do they do that often?"

"Not really, but they didn't want to go back home after the game. Especially when I have to be over there tomorrow anyway."

"They can stay the night with me and David if they want." She leans her head on my shoulder, "We can make a night of it and watch movies, play games, and anything else we can think of."

"I can't ask you to do that."

She laughs, "You didn't ask. I offered."

Nathan can hear our conversation and he stiffens at the familiarity between us. Well, screw him. "I'll ask them and see what they say."

Marisol leans over until she can see the both of us. "We're literally right here. We can hear everything you're saying."

Gabriella pushes our sister back. "The answer is yes. We would love to stay with you tonight."

"Then it's settled," Caroline adds matter of factly. "After the game, we'll grab a pizza and pick a movie."

"Yes," they both whisper.

"David will be excited." She's talking as if her son's dad isn't sitting right in front of us. As if he won't try to do something to screw this all up.

"It's our turn with the ball." I nod toward the field and watch our offense take the field. David looks much bigger than he actually is with all his pads on.

The center snaps the ball back to him, and he looks around the field, trying to find an open receiver. Finally, he sees one and throws the ball. For a split second, I think it's going to fall short, but it lands in the hands of his target. The receiver runs and gets a few yards before being tackled.

"That's my little QB." Bryce jumps up from the seat and throws his arms in the air.

We're all shouting variations of "way to go David." Everyone except Nathan. He has his arms crossed in front of him, and seems bored to be here. If he's so annoyed, I don't understand why he doesn't just leave. It'd be a hell of a lot easier on the rest of us.

I shake my thoughts free of the menace in front of us and focus on the game. I'm here for David. That is it.

Another pass and they get closer to the endzone. Two more plays and they make a touchdown. All of us jump up and cheer. It might be obnoxious, but I'd rather him know we are all here for him than to wonder if we paid attention to the game at all. He may be young, but he's not dumb.

The other team gets a touchdown and misses the field goal...barely. What are they feeding these kids? The only thing I can think of is they have private coaches who come in to help their kids. I get it. If you want your child to get a sports scholarship in a smalltown high school, the scouts need a reason to come. I just didn't realize it started this early. Shows how much I know about being a sports parent. Or, a parent in general.

Another touchdown for our team, and they block the other team from scoring again. Caroline has a tight grip on my leg. She's anxious, and I'm not sure of the reason. Is it Nathan? Or is it because she's worried about the outcome of the game? I want to ask her but there are too many listening ears.

It's halftime and Bryce leans over to tell us all the things he's worked on with David. No wonder the kid is good. His uncle was a starting quarterback his freshman year. I wonder if their mom paid for private lessons, but I don't think she did. Bryce had a natural talent and put in a lot of work. I'm sure David will do the same if he decides to stick with this sport.

"I'll be right back." Nathan stands and walks down the stairs. The rest of us shrug and go back to our conversations.

It's warm, but not so hot we can't stand being out here. A breeze blows through and Caroline snuggles into me. "He's pretty good."

"He is. Your brother's done a hell of a job helping him."

"I hope like hell he didn't hear that. He'll gloat for weeks."

Bryce grins, "Too late. Who knows maybe I'll go into coaching after I graduate."

"Lord, help us all," their mom says into the air. We all know she's joking but Bryce shakes his head.

The players run onto the field again and the second half begins. The ex-husband hasn't made his way back, and I hope David doesn't notice. Even though my dad worked weird hours when I was a kid, he always showed up to my things. If things work out with Caroline, I plan on doing the same. I want to be the stability in both of their lives. The person they know will always be there for them and do their best not to let them down.

The other team is catching up and we're on the edge of our seats as the game progresses. Bryce's knuckles turn white as he clasps his hands in front of him. Caroline is squeezing my leg, and I'm pretty sure I'll have crescent shaped marks in the exact spot.

I really hope they don't lose this game. David has such high hopes they'll win since everyone is here, and I want his team to get the victory they deserve.

They are up by one touchdown and have the ball. As long as they don't fumble it, they've got this. Seconds are left in the game, and David throws the ball. The receiver almost drops the ball, but has his hands around it. He runs toward the end zone and scores the touchdown. All of us stand, throwing our arms in the air. With the energy we have you'd think it was a major game instead of the first of a short season.

The players shake hands with the other team, and gather in the middle of the field amped about their win. The coach talks to them for a few minutes and they head off the field to their parents. We make our way down the bleachers and he runs up to Bryce. "You were right."

"Definitely never hearing the end of that," Caroline rolls her eyes and scoops her son in a hug. "You did amazing out there."

"Thanks, Mom." He looks around at the people crowded around us, "Where did dad go?"

"I'm not sure." She lets go of him and steps back. "He said he'd be right back."

David spots my sisters and runs up to them. "Y'all came!"

"Yep, and we're spending the night with you." Marisol grins and gives him a quick hug.

"Awesome. Can we go now? It's hot." He pulls at the collar of his jersey.

"Yep." Caroline walks toward the parking lot.

David holds hands with both of my sisters, and we make our way to Caroline's car. The girls will need to swing by my car and get their stuff, but that can wait a few more moments. The closer we get; I see a figure standing right next to her car. Seriously?

Nathan is leaning against the hood, trying to pull off that whole eighty's heartthrob thing. It's not working, and I don't know what he thinks he'll gain by this. He stands as Caroline walks ahead of us. "We need to talk."

"No," she shakes her head, "we really don't."

"I want to take David for the rest of the weekend."

"It's not your weekend. So, no." She rubs her forehead with one hand, and I know she's already stressing about the problems this can cause. "You can't pick and choose when you want to be a dad."

I motion to my sisters, and toss them the keys. They lower their voices, "Want to go with us to get our bags?"

David nods before casting a weary gaze in his mom's direction. He doesn't really want to leave her. He's a kid and shouldn't have to deal with this shit. I mean Tonya and her baby's dad have worked out the co-parenting thing, and they are younger than us. It shouldn't be this difficult. To ease his fear, I walk faster to stand by Caroline. "Is everything okay?"

"It's none of your business," Nathan spits out.

"It's a good thing I wasn't talking to you, then." I move between them until my eyes meet Caroline's. "You good?"

"Yeah." She stands taller, trying to be strong against this man who has a way of making her feel like shit.

"What part of this is none of your business do you not understand?" Nathan touches my shoulder, and I whirl around. The urge to hit him is there, but that's not something their son needs to see.

"The part where you're upsetting my girlfriend."

He snorts. Disgust written all over his face, and I want to punch him even more. "You mean *fake* girlfriend. I have friends all around town and they said she," he points toward Caroline, "didn't have a boyfriend prior to the night I showed up. So why don't you run back to your job and leave us to discuss our son."

I feel Reaf and Bryce move behind their sister. At least I know they are on my side. "Except that's not what you want to do. This is all a power play to make her feel like shit. She's moved on. It's time for you to take the hint. You can either be in your son's life, or not, but don't make your argument out to be something it isn't. I've shown her more love, compassion, and been there for her more than I'm sure you ever did when you were married. I've also gotten to know your son over the past couple of months. You don't get to dictate their lives anymore."

He laughs. This asshole actually laughs, as if he doesn't have a care in the world. "I'm making sure she only has our son's best interest at heart. And dating a bartender isn't it. Hell, it'd be better if she didn't date at all. David should be her only focus."

"Are you fucking kidding me right now? She's allowed to be happy. You're just pissed it's not with you even though you threw her away as soon as you were bored."

He opens his mouth, but doesn't get a chance to speak because Caroline moves between us. "She is right here and capable of speaking for herself," she points a finger at Nathan, "you need to get off my car. Go tell David goodbye, and my lawyer will be in touch on Monday."

I reach my arm out to wrap her into me, but she holds up her hand. "And you need to go. Your sisters can still stay the night. I'll drop them off in the morning, but I can't be around you right now."

"But." She crosses her arms, and I know now is not the time. I turn and there's a crowd of parents looking our direction, and I know right then...I fucked up.

27

caroline

I CAN'T BELIEVE that just happened. And with a freaking audience. Carlos is protective of me, and I like that. It makes me feel valued. At the same time...it's not his place to stand up for me to Nathan. I was handling it. What I didn't need was raised voices, and all my dirty laundry spilled in a public setting.

The other parents move toward their cars now that the show is over. Glad I could provide them some weekend entertainment. At least David wasn't over here to see the verbal sparring between Carlos and Nathan. I love that Carlos's sisters took him with them to get their things.

I watch Carlos as he walks across the lot to his own car. His head is down and I kind of feel bad for snapping at him, but this was not the time or place to have that conversation. He stops at the edge of his car and bends down to give David a high five and hug. He tells his sisters goodbye then gets in his car and leaves.

Before the kids make it to us, my mom and brothers

surround me. "Everything will work out," Mom pats my shoulder, "you need time to cool off and so does he."

"I know." I lean against my car and make sure David isn't around us. "But how do I know he won't do something like that again when it comes to Nathan? I don't want it to be something David sees even though his dad is shitty."

Reaf moves beside me and puts his arm over my shoulder. "Look, I can't guarantee it won't happen again, but...if you mean that much to him, he'll figure out when he needs to be silent. It was hard for me when I got with Tonya. Layla's dad was horrible then. But he's changed. I know that ship has most likely sailed for Nathan, but it could be what brings him in to be a better father to David."

"That's a lot of coulds and ifs." I run my hand over my hair. It would be more satisfying if it wasn't in a ponytail. "I just don't want to get serious with him and this become a normal thing."

Mom laughs, "Sweetie, it's been serious with him for a bit. You need to quit lying to yourself."

My brother shakes his head and looks over at me. "I know it's scary letting him in all the way. You need to talk to him and tell him your expectations when it comes to dealing with Nathan." I open my mouth but he stops me. "You also need to get more consistent with your boundaries when it comes to Nathan running over you. Today is the first time I've seen you really stand up to him. As long as he knows the lines he can't cross, everything will work out."

"Did Tonya do the same thing to you?"

"Yeah," he sighs, "she's had me wrapped around her finger since early on in our relationship."

"Clearly it's not an issue for you."

"Hell no, it isn't. I'll do whatever she asks with a smile on my face. And I think Carlos would do the same for you."

He's got a point but I can't say anything else about it

because David and the girls are in hearing range. "Are y'all ready to go?"

Carlos's sisters look nervously at each other. I know they can feel the tension and want to know what happened. They won't hear it from me, though. Carlos is their brother, and it's not my place to say anything. "Yeah," Gabi smiles. "My brother wants to know if he needs to leave a key out for us in the morning."

This is...more awkward than I thought it would be. He usually comes over for breakfast with us in the mornings before he heads to his mom's or work. We've already fallen into a routine with him and this interruption will be difficult. "Probably, just in case."

"I'll text him." Marisol pulls her phone out of her pocket and taps on the screen. "So, pizza?"

"Yes, definitely pizza." And I hope like hell they don't judge me because I'll be having wine with mine.

We hug my mom and brothers, telling them goodbye before piling into my car. "We'll stop and grab the pizza on the way home. Start thinking about what movies y'all want to watch."

All three of them sit in the backseat with David in the middle. I pull out of my spot and start driving toward downtown. "Just don't let her talk you into her weird vampire and werewolf love stories." David groans and I feel bad for making him endure my favorite movies.

"What?" Marisol gasps. "You don't like vampires and werewolves?"

"Not really."

"They're our favorite." Gabriella adds before listing off her favorite movies.

David puts his head in his hands and groans. "Dang it. That's what we're watching isn't it?"

"We'll see," Marisol looks up and winks at me through the rearview mirror.

Her familiarity with me is amazing and will make it that much more heartbreaking if I can't make Carlos understand why what happened earlier wasn't good. It was everything that needed to be said, but not the right time. Tonight, though, I'm going to enjoy the time I have with his sisters. Even though he gripes about them, they are funny. And they include David in all their conversations. I couldn't ask for better people to be in his corner.

Let's hope they continue to stay there. Even if things don't work out the way I'm hoping.

* * *

While I'd like to say David lost and we got to watch all the vampire swooniness? That's not what happened. Marisol and Gabriella thought it would be mean if they came and interrupted his day of victory. So, we're watching another superhero movie. Thank goodness it's almost over because we've seen it like a thousand times already.

While they finish the movie, I get up and head to my bedroom. I have a few board games tucked away in the back of my closet. We only get them out whenever my brothers and mom come over because some of them are just no fun when there's only two players.

I pull out Monopoly and Sorry. Both are games that are sure to piss everyone off, but in a fun way.

Closing the closet door behind me, I glance at my phone on the nightstand. Before we started the movie, hell before we ate, I decided it was best to put it in here. Otherwise, I would have the urge to text Carlos or see whatever bullshit Nathan is blowing up my phone with.

The pull to check it is strong. But so am I.

I'll text Nathan tomorrow and let him know if he's going to act like an asshole, he's not welcome at any of David's games. If I have to get a court order to make it happen, I will. I'm done playing these stupid little games Nathan wants to play because he wants to have some sort of control over me. I'm over it. We haven't been together in years. And honestly, I'm a little sick of myself for putting up with it for that long.

My brother was right. I've never stood up to him. Not until today. And I intend on keeping those boundaries in place. Not only are they healthy for me, but they are healthy for David. His dad can pick him up on his appointed weekends and days or he can't see him. Those are the only options. Plus, he can't tell me he'll take me back to court because that is what the papers say. One night a week and every other weekend.

Carlos...well, that's an entirely different conversation. Both of us need to cool down and get our heads on straight. Because what happened today after the game and cannot happen ever again.

When Nathan left me, I was the ass end of everybody's jokes. Because somehow it was my fault that I couldn't keep my husband. I've worked damn hard to make sure I don't give people a reason to gossip about me since then. All I know is I don't want this to be the thing that breaks us.

I'm in love with him, and have been since the day he put me on the counter so I wouldn't cut my feet on the glass. It helps that I also had a crush on him before he ever asked me out. But he doesn't know that, or need to.

"Mom." David pokes his head in the door. I didn't realize I've almost made it to my nightstand. "Are you coming?"

"I'll be there in a second. Can you get the table cleaned off so we can play in there?"

"Yes, ma'am." He trusts that I'll be right behind him, and takes off toward the front of the house.

My phone lights up and I reach for it, but don't pick it up. I will not do this tonight. One day, that's all I need to get my thoughts under control. Then maybe I can finally tell Carlos how I feel about him. How I have for weeks.

"Come on, Mom." David hollers loud enough for me to hear him.

I don't bother answering, and hurry into the kitchen with the games. All three kids are sitting at the table when I walk in. A drink sitting in front of each of them. They have a wine glass in front of my chair. I'm not sure if I should be offended or not.

I hold both games in the air, "So which do we want to play?"

"Literally anything other than Monopoly." Gabriella takes a drink. "If we start that one, we'll be here all night."

"You're right, and I definitely don't want to do that." I turn and toss that game onto the couch. "Set this up while I pour myself a glass of wine."

David takes the game out of the box, and the girls get all the small pieces, shuffle the cards and wait until I'm back to pick colors. "I want to go first." Of course, he does.

"You always go first," I motion toward Marisol and Gabriella, "why don't we let our guests do the honors this time?"

"It's okay, Caroline." Gabi grins up at me.

"Yeah." Marisol adds. "Today is his day after that awesome game. Who knows? Maybe if he goes first, he'll pull off another win."

"You two aren't helping his ego, at all."

Both of them laugh and set their pieces in the start area. "Let's get this game going."

We're halfway through the board, David is of course winning, when there's a knock at the door. I wasn't expecting anyone. Reaf and Tonya have a date night and Mom is watching Layla. Bryce is God knows where before he heads back to school.

Pushing the chair back, I get up and walk toward the front door. The girls have gone quiet, and keep shooting glances in my direction. Before my hand is even on the knob, I have a gut feeling about who it is.

I take two deep breaths, turn the knob before pulling it open. Just as I suspected...Carlos is standing in front of me. "What are you doing here?"

"Can, uh, you come outside for a second?" He won't look me in the eyes, and whatever I say now will set the tone between us. "I need to talk to you."

All three kids look at the board when I turn their direction. Yeah, this conversation can't be had here. Not when they will listen to every word. "Keep playing, and skip me. Okay?"

The three of them nod, and David pulls a card from the deck. If the girls try to listen in, my kid will snitch. He has no problem tattling.

I walk through the door and close it behind me. It's dark out here, and I'm glad for the cover. My emotions will be hidden, but so will his. The chair at the farthest edge of the porch is calling my name and I make my way toward it.

He follows behind and sits in the chair on the other side of the table. A reversal of how we sat out here that one night. When Nathan spilled the beans about Carlos to David. This time he doesn't have ice cream, and I can't help but think that's a bad omen.

Leaning forward with his elbows on his knees, he clasps his hands in front of him. "I wanted to apologize for today. I should have kept my mouth shut. It's not my place to intervene when it comes to your ex-husband."

"You're correct. I told you I had it, but you wouldn't stop." I lean back in my chair, my head hanging over the back.

"Do you realize how weak I felt not being given the chance to defend myself or decisions to him?"

"I'm sorry," he says again. "But I couldn't let him talk about you the way he was. Not about the woman I love." His mouth snaps shut. He didn't mean to say that.

"Wh—what was that?" I want to make sure I heard him right.

"I said." He clears his throat, "I couldn't let him bash the woman I love. And I understand if you don't love me back. I also understand if you want to break up with me because I was out of line. It wasn't the time."

"Did you go to work tonight?" If he's this frazzled right now, I can't imagine him being behind the bar serving drinks. Also, I'm curious.

He shakes his head and stares at his shoes. "I went to talk to my mom. She scolded me, and told me to figure it out. That I 'better not do anything to ruin this relationship and to try at all costs to win you back.' She wasn't very nice about it, either."

"Did you really need to be told that?"

"Not even a little bit. I was going to wait until morning and show up with breakfast, but I couldn't. I had to let you know that you're it for me."

"I—." I begin but he holds up a hand.

"Hold on, I have something for you." He jumps out of his chair and rushes to his car. He has something in his hands, and gives it to me. "It might be melted, but my sisters said ice cream helps everything."

"So does wine." I laugh and open the container. The ice cream is definitely melted, and it drips down the side of the carton. Setting both of them down on the table, I stand and our eyes meet. "I know we won't figure everything out at once, but until I get things squared away with Nathan, I need you to let me fight my own battles."

He opens his mouth, but I put a finger over his lips. "I love you, too. I have for a while if I'm being honest. I was just too scared to admit it to myself."

"Those are the best words I've heard all day." He leans down until his lips meet mine. He's the only person that makes me feel safe despite whatever arguments we have. In all honesty, this wasn't a huge one, but it's important that he knows where I stand.

Our tongues mingle, and it feels perfect. Like I'm home.

"Grownups are gross." We both hear David and jump apart from each other. He isn't the only one standing in the door. Marisol and Gabriela are standing at his side.

"I thought y'all were playing the game."

"You were taking too long. We thought we'd see if you were okay." Marisol's wolf grin tells me she's full of crap, but I'll allow it.

"We're coming in." I grab the melted ice cream and head toward the door. "How bad am I losing?"

"It's not good, Mom." Leave it to him to be a bubble of optimism.

"I think now is a good time for us to play Monopoly." Gabi smiles. "That will tell us if the two of you can truly withstand anything."

"Kids." Carlos groans. He follows me inside.

We set up the game in the living room. I have a feeling it's going to get rowdy, but it's all worth it.

epilogue

THE FOOTBALL SEASON is almost over, and it's the homecoming game. The high school had theirs weeks ago, but since the little league got a late start, it's time now. The cheerleaders are dressed up and wearing mums, ready to cheer on their team.

Caroline is sitting next to me on the bleachers. Her family is in the row in front of us, and my mom is on my other side. A special presentation is about to start. The football players are being lead down the field with their parents or cheerleaders.

David, of course, didn't want either to walk him onto the field. He was worried about hurting his dad's feelings by asking me in case he didn't show up. Caroline respected his wishes, even though I think she's a tad bit heartbroken.

"It's almost his turn," she whispers in my ear.

He's the last one to come on the field since he's the star quarterback. Bryce's words not David's. Though I have noticed David walks around a bit taller. They've only lost one game all season, and he's not shy about letting people know.

Finally, they call David onto the field. He's on the fifty-yard line with Marisol on one arm and Gabriela on the other. Both of them are in Asheville's colors wearing mums made by Tonya and Caroline. They are almost as big as them. The flower covers their entire upper body and the ribbons flow down past their knees. Caroline had to add a ribbon so they could hang them around their necks. I've never understood why they need to be so massive.

His grin is wide as they make their way toward the front of the field, and Caroline is snapping pictures like it's his senior year in high school. After he makes it down, the National Anthem is played and we all sit to watch the game.

Out of the corner of my eye, I see Nathan walking up the bleachers. He doesn't try to sit beside us, though. He's on the opposite side in the visitor section. At least he's here and not trying to start anything with Caroline this time.

We watch the game. I'd like to say it was a close one, but we demolished the other team. David runs out to us after the coach's talk at the end. We stay in the bleachers. There's no use bumping into other parents to get to him faster.

Before I realize it, David is wrapping his arms around Caroline, almost knocking her over. "Did you see all my passes? They were amazing!"

"They sure were," she laughs.

Nathan slowly makes his way over to us. I learned my lesson last time. If he says anything, I'll be quiet. He waits for David to make his rounds before getting his attention. "That was a great game, Buddy."

"You came!" David crushes his dad in a hug. "I can't wait for the next game."

"I'll do my best to be there." He squeezes him and kisses him on top of the head. "I'll let you get back to your celebration. One weekend soon, I'll pick you up if it's okay with your mom."

He glances at her then me. "As long as it's on your weekend, I'm fine with it. And you have to have him home at a decent time."

"I can do that." He ruffles David's hair and walks off.

"That was unexpected." I say softly enough that only Caroline hears.

"I know. But I'm not holding my breath. He always tells him one thing and does something different."

I've seen it for myself. But I have this badass woman by my side who is capable of handling anything with, or without, me.

"Why don't we go out to eat and celebrate?" I ask everyone.

"Yes," David yells. "I'm starving."

"I bet you are," Caroline rolls her eyes, "but first you have to go home and shower. You stink."

"Fine."

All of us make our way down the bleachers. Caroline grabs my hand and this is exactly how it's supposed to be. It looks like I got the kind of relationship my parents had after all. There may be bumps in the road, but as long as we stick with it, we can do this for the long haul.

acknowledgments

Wee One and Boy Child, I love you. You are the best parts of my life, and I can't wait to see where your journeys lead you.

My friends and family, y'all are amazing! I love you to the edges of the universe. Thank you for understanding when I have to turn things down because I'm writing.

The team behind my books. I couldn't do this without you. I would literally be lost without your support. Thank you for standing by me. You have no idea how much I appreciate you.

My Alphas, y'all rock. Seriously...don't let anyone tell you differently.

Readers, you make my world go round. Anytime you find a book boyfriend in any of my books, it gives me rush. Thank you for sticking with me all these years and taking a chance on my books.

also by katrina marie

Cousins Gone RomCom Series

Cocktails & Crushes

Brews & Bartenders

Gone in Love Series

The Taking Chances Series

Cocky Hero Club

Big Baller

Baseball & Broadway

about the author

Katrina Marie lives in the Dallas area with her husband, two children, and two fur babies. She is a lover of all things geeky and nerdy. When she's not writing you can find her at her children's sporting events, or curled up reading a book.

You can find Katrina Marie online in the following places:
Sign up for my newsletter: https://www.subscribepage.com/
KatrinaMarieNewsletter
Website: katrinamarieauthor.com

facebook.com/katrinamarieauthor

twitter.com/katmarieauthor

instagram.com/katrinamarieauthor

bookbub.com/profile/katrina-marie

pinterest.com/katrinamarieauthor

tiktok.com/@katrinamarieauthor

patreon.com/katrinamarie